A selection of recent titles by Guy N. Smith

MANEATER
THE CADAVER
NIGHT OF THE CRABS
CRABS' FURY
DEADBEAT
NIGHTSPAWN
THE EIGHTH DAY

www.guynsmith.com
@guynsmith

Psalm 151

GUY N SMITH

BLACK HILL BOOKS

First Published in eBook format by
Black Hill Books, England, August 2013.

First Published in Paperback format by
Black Hill Books, England, August 2013.

FIRST EDITION

ISBN: 1907846840
ISBN-13: 978-1-907846-84-7

Dedicated to Ashley Davis in appreciation of her excellent proof reading.

Lichfield District Council

This Certificate is Awarded to

Guy N. Smith

Shortlisted Author in the 1993 Lichfield Prize
for the novel 'Psalm 151'.

James Redshaw Ltd
Booksellers

ORION

Signed: ....
Chief Executive of Lichfield District Council

....
Chairman of Lichfield District Council

1993 Lichfield Prize Shortlist Certificate

PART ONE – SUMMER

1

Herbert Poppleton boasted, not with an arrogance that hinted at superiority over his fellow men but with an undisguised pride, that in fifty-one years of marriage neither he nor his late wife, God rest her soul, had ever viewed each other unclothed. Theirs had been the perfect marriage, absolute fidelity, love and affection that had not paled over the years.

Her devotion had been unstinted. He remembered how, in 1956 when he was first appointed organist at Lichfield Cathedral, Maude had saved from her pittance of a housekeeping allowance in order that he might buy a suit that was equal to his status. Charcoal grey with pin stripes and a waistcoat that strained at the buttons; it still hung in his wardrobe, shiny and impregnated with mothballs. The buttons would no longer fasten; two had popped when he had tried it on in one of his frequent moods of sad nostalgia. Otherwise, he would have worn it on Sundays for evensong.

All his suits had to be made to measure; his unfortunate figure had never permitted him to buy one off the tailor's rack. Short in stature, he had been 5ft 4in when he had achieved his degree in music, and doubtless he had shrunk since then. His body was ill proportioned; his large balding head was a burden to his narrow shoulders, his stomach has always protruded even though he had always eaten frugally, and his short legs gave him an almost dwarf-like appearance in contrast to his long arms. As a consolation, and he had no wish to criticise his maker, he thought that he might have been endowed with aristocratic features; he had no wish to be handsome.

Instead, his nose was bulbous, his eyes were small and buried in fleshy sockets, magnified hideously by the thick-lensed glasses, which he had been compelled to wear since childhood. A hair lip added a touch of grotesqueness. All of which combined to make him reclusive and short-tempered.

Yet he had always been loving and gentle with Maude. Hardly a cross word had been exchanged in over half a century. But he blamed himself for her death, the stroke that had snatched her from within a year of their retirement from cathedral duties.

He had had no option but to retire. With an organist at eighty the cathedral was looking for a younger man, any mistakes which he made whilst playing the organ were due to his failing eyesight and not to his musical skills. Stronger lenses and increased lighting had not helped. Far better, as Bishop Franklin had put it to him in that holy man's inimitable way, to retire at one's peak than to go into decline. No previous organist held such a record of never having missed a service for fifty years and it was unlikely that Poppleton's impeccable and devoted service to the cathedral would ever be surpassed. He was a legend in his own lifetime; he would be remembered for posterity. In due course they would erect a plaque to his memory in the organ loft.

So Herbert had agreed to retire. It was the most difficult decision of his life. The Dean and Chapter were agreeable to himself and Maude remaining in their small house in Vicar's Close for the rest of their days. It was a tempting offer. Herbert and Maude talked it over. This place had been their home since 1956, but to stay here in the shadow of the cathedral might prove distressing for Herbert; in summer when the west doors were left open the strains of the organ could be clearly heard. The music would not be Herbert's, it would be stressful and hurtful, and a reminder that another had replaced him in the only role in life that he had ever wanted.

Herbert and Maude agreed that it would be best for them to leave Lichfield, never to return. Not even for memorial services. They contemplated a coastal retirement home, decided against it. Seaside resorts were bleak and lonely places during the winter months. Suppose one of them died. No, that was a long way off yet; they needed only each other, they did not need to cultivate outside friendships. They had no friends in the Close, only acquaintances. It would always be that way.

Herbert chose Malvern. Because of Elgar, principally. And Shaw had lived there, too. It would be a fitting place for one whose organ compositions and recitals had earned him such accolade in a cathedral city. He and Maude would be able to enjoy occasional walks in the hills and it was reputed that the water had cured many an ailment. Maude would benefit from that.

Maude died eleven months to the day when they moved to their small town house. That morning she showed no outward signs of feeling unwell; by afternoon she was dead.

Herbert was plagued by the belief that had they remained in their former home and its tranquil surrounds, she would have been alive today. The move had distressed her, but she had concealed her unhappiness from him as she had often done over minor things in the past. She had pined and died.

He decided against returning to Lichfield. At eighty-five, he surely had not much time left. He grieved in solitude, passed the days listening to Beethoven and Mozart recitals on the record player, which Maude had given to him as a wedding present. Sometimes, during the summer months, he took short walks up into the hills; the magnificent solitude gave him a sense of being close to Maude. He spoke with her the way he always used to, discussed Bach, his all-time favourite. He had never discovered whether or not Maude shared his love of the great composers; if she didn't, then she certainly engaged upon intelligent discussions with him, and he loved her for her selflessness.

Today he felt closer than ever to his dearly departed wife. It was as though Maude walked at his side, the tip tapping of the silver-headed cane, which he had carried for five decades, her footsteps alongside his own.

That cane was as much a part of his image as the tightly fitting suit, the last one which Jackson, the city tailor, had made before he sold out to a nationwide chain of clothiers.

The small highly polished stick had been found on one of the pews by Homer, the Head Verger, after a military memorial service. An officer's without doubt, maybe a high-ranking one. Under normal circumstances it would have been handed in as lost property. Poppleton had told the Verger he would see to it; he had, and he had carried it in full view ever since. If the rightful owner had put in a claim, Herbert would have given it back to him. There had been no such claim and the organist was still minding it fifty years hence. It wasn't like *stealing*, was it? Just *borrowing*. All the same, its possession still pricked his conscience.

Maude might even have been walking with him today. It was hot, oppressive; the sweat beaded on his extensive forehead, trickled down into his eyes, made them smart and distorted his fading vision even more than usual. He did not mind because he had his wife alongside him, on parole from God.

Before long they would rest, find somewhere to sit down, talk about Bach and Mozart and the Lichfield years. Maude would enjoy that.

He was sure that there were people in close proximity, could just discern their outlines as if they stood in a fog or heat haze. Water splashed, gurgled.

Herbert knew where he was now, up by the spring that gushed out of the hillside through an iron pipe, filled and overflowed a stone trough. Icy cold pure water—there were always folk here filling containers from it, about the only thing that was free apart from the fresh air up here. Health-giving water that would possibly have cured Maude of her arthritis had she lived long enough to reap its benefits. One could buy it in bottles from the shops, of course, at some astronomical price. Herbert Poppleton's pension hadn't run to that. Again he felt a twinge of guilt. Had he made sacrifices in other areas and bought the spa water, then Maude might still be here.

But she was here.

Somebody spoke to him; he raised his cane in an

acknowledgement. He was too breathless to reply, and he had no wish to indulge in idle conversation. Back in the old days in the Close he always spoke with his stick when the pupils from the Cathedral School waved to him. Sometimes he grunted an unintelligible reply. Some of the boys were choristers in the cathedral, he took them for choir practice every day in the Song School. He was very fond of them in contrast to his abrupt manner.

He would have to rest soon; his short legs ached their complaint. There was a bench seat just off the rough track; it commanded a panoramic view of the Worcestershire countryside. It was so elevated that once he had experienced a touch of vertigo. He would not today, though, because his vision was blurred and reduced. He had not even been able to discern the features of those people by the spring and they had only been a few yards away.

Nevertheless, a sit down would be most welcome.

It took him some time to find the seat; he had already passed it, realized it when the path ended abruptly in some gorse bushes, and retraced his steps. Miraculously on a day like today, it wasn't occupied. He sighed his relief as he sank down on to its weather-beaten slats, closed his eyes momentarily. He was sure Maude was sitting alongside him. He was frightened to glance sideways in case she wasn't, it would be cruel to disillusion himself.

He often talked aloud to himself, a habit that his long-suffering wife had endured over the years; she knew that he did not appreciate being disturbed in his ramblings. So he talked on now as he used to then; about the composers, his own compositions, the one which he had had published and never been paid for, but money was a small consideration where the arts were concerned.

He squinted out at the view but all he saw was a grey mist that reflected the bright sunshine and dazzled him.

He might have dozed, he could not be sure. All he knew was that he seemed to have been here for a very long time. He started, fumbled for his pocket watch. He always liked to be home by four, he had tea at 4.30. He was still governed by diocesan routine. Evensong was sung at 5.30, Monday to Friday. Rigid discipline still ruled his weekdays. Goodness, he ought to be going. It was 3.45 and it was a full forty-five minutes' walk home from here.

That was when he realized that there was somebody else sitting on the bench beside him. A shape in a cataract fog, a form that huddled just the way Maude used to sit, leaning forward when her head drooped with drowsiness; she always slept sitting upright on the sofa.

It *was* Maude.

"Good afternoon, Mr Poppleton."

It *wasn't* Maude.

Disappointment. Disillusionment. The dream had become reality and that was cruel.

"I beg your pardon, sir."

"It is Mr Poppleton, isn't it?" A man's voice, a baritone if he was a singer. Cultured. Not curious, because the question was only confirmation seeking, a means of introduction. The face was turned towards him but it was hidden in grey shadow, featureless.

"Yes, yes." Impatience and annoyance. Herbert did not encourage conversation with strangers; if anybody spoke to him in the Italian restaurant where he dined on Sundays, he ignored them. But out here, amidst the rolling hills, that was more difficult. "Do I know you?"

"You did once, many years ago, but I could not be so presumptuous as to ask if you remember me. Hundreds of choirboys have passed through your hands, I'm sure. Suffice it to say that I know you and quite by chance we have met on a deserted hillside. I remember your wife, too."

"She passed away eleven months after we moved out here." Herbert's voice was husky; he fumbled for his watch again. "Tea is at – 4:30. I can't be late."

"No, I'm sure you can't," – he gave a hint of a laugh – "but not to worry. My car's only a hundred yards down the track; I can give you a lift back into town. I presume that you do live in town?"

"Yes. Along by the Winter Gardens."

"A lovely position, I'm sure. I'm sorry to hear about your wife, I do recall her. She always wore a large hat and a veil. As schoolboys, we used to live in awe of her."

"That was her," – sadness again – "I'm glad you remember her. I'm sorry; I didn't catch your name?"

"It wouldn't mean anything to you, sir. But I'll never forget your playing in the cathedral; I wish I had a record or CD of it."

"I've got one at home." Poppleton hesitated. "They presented me with a tape of an organ recital I gave during the last Lichfield Festival. But I only have one copy. If on another occasion you would care to come along with the means to copy it, I would be only too happy. Two copies, in fact, because I don't know how to do it. I'm thinking of trying but I'd hate to think of my precious original being damaged or lost."

"That can be arranged." The misty silhouetted head nodded, the face was surely smiling. "Now, we'd better make a move, I'd hate for you to be late for tea."

Herbert allowed himself to be helped up onto his feet, leaned against the other whilst he got his balance, groped for his cane.

"I see you've still got the cane, sir. I remember how you threatened to give us six of the best with it that time when some of the boys made a slide in the snow down that sloping path to the Song School, and when you came along for choir practice at midday …"

"I don't remember." Herbert was suddenly abrupt. "Now I don't wish to seem ungrateful, but time is ticking on."

"Just hold on to my arm, sir, the car's only just down the track there."

Poppleton tottered unsteadily even with his support. He wasn't at all good on his legs these days, but he supposed you couldn't ask a lot of them at eighty-five. He would not walk this far again.

"Here's the car, sir. Now, if you just hold on here, I'll go round and open the passenger door and help you in."

It was a smallish car, a garish red; by the feel of the metal, it had been recently waxed. Herbert did not know what make it was, and he didn't care; cars had never interested him. He sank down into the seat; there was plenty of room in which to stretch out his short legs.

"It's very hot in here, doesn't the window open?"

Habitual irritability, he had never tolerated discomfort or inconvenience.

"I'll put it down for you," – the other reached across him – "and you'd better put your seat belt on, too."

Herbert did not like seat belts, either. They gave him the feeling of being a prisoner. Still, he must not be too ungrateful. He wondered who this fellow was, faces came and went in his memory; many of them he knew, but could not put a name to. If only he could see the face clearly. He turned his head but the other was looking away from him. It didn't matter.

"Do you still play, sir?" The engine stuttered into life, the chassis rattled ominously.

"A little. The piano; I don't have access to an organ."

"That's a pity."

"Anything less than the cathedral organ would be an insult to the great composers."

"Of course." The car reversed out onto the track, the gears grated.

"Evensong was always my favourite, sir."

"Mine, too. And Mrs Poppleton's, she always attended."

"Do you ever play the Psalms, sir?" The question was direct, more than just idle conversation.

"Well, no, not on the piano. It would be pointless."

"Not even Psalm 151, sir?"

That was when Herbert Poppleton almost fainted, seemed to slump back in his seat, his eyes closing.

"Did you hear what I said, sir?" The driver shouted as if

he needed to make himself heard above the noise of the engine.

There was no reply.

The car bumped its way slowly down the steep, rutted road, passed a queue of people with polythene containers by the water trough. They glanced up, idly watched the vehicle until it was lost from view around a sharp bend. Some kind man had brought his aging father out for an afternoon ride in the hills, but the heatwave had proven too much for the old man, so they were going back home, or perhaps in search of a shady place to park up.

That was the last time Herbert Poppleton was seen alive.

2

The small bookshop smelled much the same as most second-hand bookshops: a dry mustiness that tickled the throat and irritated sensitive lungs, an aroma of long unopened tomes, a dusty atmosphere that was highlighted by a shaft of afternoon sunshine through the street window, illuminating an otherwise gloomy interior where the only lighting was a single unshaded 60-watt bulb suspended from the flaking ceiling.

The floor was uncarpeted so that browsers' footsteps echoed, a failsafe in case the proprietor, lurking in some backroom, had failed to hear the harsh clang of the doorbell.

There was an assortment of volumes crammed on to the shelves that lined the walls, bowed them alarmingly. The residue, designated as 'bargains', were piled on a central trestle table, an untidy motley of split bindings and scuffed covers. Beneath these were an array of cardboard boxes, spilling out their contents, thumbed and dog-eared, well-read run-of-the-mill paperbacks; £1 each or four for £3.50. The handwritten card had fallen off and lay on the floor. Possibly the bulk of the stock had been compiled over a period of time from charity shops and car boot sales.

The newcomer stood just inside the doorway hesitantly, licked his thin lips nervously, ran his fingers through a shock of grey hair. He glanced back at the partly open door, maybe wondering if he could leave before the bookseller appeared and thus save himself from the embarrassment of having to make an excuse. *I don't think I've the time to browse now; I'll come back tomorrow. Or, I'm really looking for something more specialised, antiquarian, you know.*

His figure was stooped, as though he suffered from some spinal disability; the carrier bag in his hand appeared to unbalance him with its empty wine bottle destined for the bottle bank on the nearby car park. In spite of the warmth, an unbelted, unfashionable fawn mackintosh was draped over his tweed sports jacket, complete with its elbow pads. Clean but frugal, his appearance bespoke bachelorhood, lacked the touch of a caring female.

He had half turned away when a deep, cultured voice stopped him, had his lower lip quivering like a shoplifter caught in the act.

"Can I help you?"

He turned back, squinted through the gloom at the figure which was framed in the doorway of the adjoining room. The other was small and lithe, craggy features belied an accurate guess at his age, although he must have been in his early fifties. The eyes were a shade too close together, giving an appearance of shiftiness, and a long ridged tongue traced a path along thin lips. He, it seemed, was also nervous.

"I … er … you see …" The customer searched in vain for a plausible excuse for not staying, curiosity alone had prompted him to push open the door; books were irresistible to him. He seldom bought any, except in auctions to furnish his small postal trade from home, which provided him with a meagre existence. There would be nothing here for him; he specialised in literary and theological works.

"Your face is familiar." The bookseller came down the steps, hunched his shoulders, peered. "Excuse me if I'm mistaken, but I could swear you were once a colleague of mine at the Cathedral School. I was there from '68 to '74. Drinkwater's the name. James Drinkwater."

"Drinkwater! Of course. Clay's my name. Cecil Clay."

The bottle in the carrier clinked on the floor; Clay's hand was outstretched. "What an absolutely unbelievable coincidence that we should meet in a bookshop after all these years."

In spite of their enthusiasm, the handshake was limp. A moment of embarrassed silence, and then Drinkwater said, "I've just put the kettle on upstairs. Come on up for a cup of tea, if you've got time."

Clay followed the other up a narrow flight of stairs; he half wished that he had refused the invitation. An impetuous decision—he never socialised; ever since his parents had died he had lived alone in the small family home on the outskirts of the city. He had his books and his music, a degree in English Literature at Oxford. He had never asked for anything else from life.

"My humble abode." Drinkwater indicated the untidy room, the cluttered desk and the unmade bed, books stacked around the skirting boards. A cordless kettle was steaming on a tin tray. "Tea or coffee?"

"Whichever you're making, Drinkwater." Clay lapsed into the use of the surname; seldom had first names been used at the school in the Close. It had all been part of the rigid discipline.

"I always drink tea." Drinkwater reached down two mugs and a packet of teabags. Out of the corner of his eye, he saw how his visitor was scrutinising a painting of a girl's head on a wooden board that hung from an upright beam. "I picked that up in a junk shop in London for a quid. Quite attractive, isn't she?"

"Absolutely marvellous." Long fair hair that had a soft texture even on wood, eyes that saw you, held your gaze, wouldn't let you go. Seduction in oils, the full red lips mimed words that you found yourself straining to catch, whispers that faded before you heard them. "Extremely erotic, if you don't mind me saying, Drinkwater."

"Not at all, but I find the artwork more interesting. I wonder if she was a model or just a figment of the artist's imagination. The work has an unsurpassed beauty that comes to life." He held out a mug of tea. "And what are you doing with yourself these days, Cecil?"

"Er … very little." Clay's hands shook, slopped some of the dark brown fluid. "My father died in '90, my mother in '93. I've kept the house on. I do a little bookselling to pay the bills."

"Oh?" Drinkwater's eyebrows arched. "A fellow

tradesman, eh?"

"Oh, no, no, nothing like that really." Clay was afraid in case he had trespassed upon the other's livelihood. "I buy literature and theological books, sell a few by post. That's all."

"I just sell rubbish." Drinkwater laughed to put the other at ease. "If I pick up a book for fifty pence and get a quid for it, I'm happy. A bit of a sideline to subsidise a Vicar Choral's meagre allowance. The shop was on a reasonable lease; basically I wanted the living accommodation, such as it is." The deprecating hand waved again. "It's adequate. I'm not the marrying type."

"Me, neither." Clay dropped his gaze as if he was embarrassed again, stole another glance at that painting. "I collect pictures, too. That's as far as I've ever got to having a relationship with a member of the opposite sex. Tell me, Drinkwater …"

"Call me James and I'll call you Cecil." The formalities were becoming irritating.

"Right, Drink … James, I mean. Where did you go after the Cathedral School?"

"Wrekin. My father died and my mother couldn't afford to send me to university. I wasn't clever enough to win a scholarship. I auditioned for Canterbury, didn't make it. A few jobs kept me going and then, last year, I auditioned for Vicar Choral at the cathedral here and was accepted. It's hard going, but I'm keeping abreast of it. I must say, though," – a whimsical smile – "life hasn't changed much in the Close. It's a kind of backwater, like a select club. You keep your nose clean and they'll look after you. They don't like outsiders; they try to ban visitors' cars from the Close. There's a move afoot to bring in wheel clamping! Just imagine, an old boy of the school like ourselves paying a visit to the Cathedral. He leaves a fiver in the offertory box and when he comes out he's got to pay a hundred quid to get his car unclamped!"

"Scandalous." Clay nodded his head, sipped his tea

noisily, and was reminded that he had not used a deodorant that morning. Because he had not expected to socialise. Thank goodness bookshops smelled like they always did. "Is Wilson still alive?"

"The tyrant headmaster." Drinkwater grimaced. "If he is, then he doesn't deserve to be. Two of the best for forgetting to put your football boots away after games, four for not paying attention in his Latin class, and six for being late for a cathedral service. *His* priorities. My ass used to look like a zebra!"

"Archaic." Cecil Clay pursed his lips. "I've lived in the city all my life, but you don't hear much of the old Close hierarchy. Except for Poppleton, of course."

"Oh yes, I did read about it in the papers a few weeks back. Dreadful business, some nutter topped him."

"They …" Clay glanced around as though he feared lest somebody might be listening, his voice dropped to a whisper. "They …" He swallowed, blanched. "They cut off his *whatsit*, you know!"

"Oh, dear." Drinkwater's fingers trembled on the handle of his mug, "I didn't know that. How dreadful. I read that his body was discovered in some undergrowth on the Malvern Hills where he had gone to retire. He must've been a good age."

"Eighty-five."

"Some sicko, doubtless. A motiveless killing for the sake of it. Still, I suppose it's better than murdering some young girl with her life still in front of her."

"But why Herbert Poppleton?"

"Who knows? He just happened to be in the wrong place at the wrong time when this bloke had got his bloodlust up. I haven't heard that the police have got anybody for it."

"They haven't." Cecil Clay shook his head slowly, respect for the dead and a criticism of law and order. "It was on Crimewatch UK. They're looking for a chap between forty and fifty who was seen driving a red Ford Focus. The car was stolen, abandoned in Cornwall. The owner lived in

Birmingham. Apart from that, the trail is growing colder by the day. Myself, I doubt they'll get him. Unless he strikes again."

"Herbert was a nice guy when you got to know him." Drinkwater carried his empty mug across to the sink. "You remember the Song School days, don't you, Cecil?"

"Indeed, I do. Some of the boys made a slide down the sloping drive one snowy day. Herbert travelled the length of it on his backside. We queued to watch through the keyhole."

"I must've been absent on that occasion, I bet it was a sight."

"We paid for it. An extra choir practice and he got us all six of the best from Wilson."

"Remember how he used to invite us round to his house for tea and scones individually? A kind of reward, I suppose, for having to stay on at school until after Christmas. His missus was a strange bird, always wore a veil, I never ever saw her face. Apart from sitting in the rear pews for services, she was even more of a recluse than he was. When you went to the house, you never saw her. There was a plate of scones and a pot of tea put in the lounge; you heard her moving around upstairs, then silence. Like she had gone for a lie down."

"I only ever went there once." Cecil blushed; he was trembling slightly. "Who is the organist now? As I said, you don't get to know much about the cathedral unless you're a regular in the congregation or part of the Close Clique."

"A guy named Frame. Rupert Frame. He's *okay,* that's about all you can say about him. He plays well, does a good job, no fuss. No personality. I guess that's what they want today, not a living legend that goes on for fifty years. I've only ever seen his wife once, she keeps a low profile, doesn't get involved. I don't care much for the assistant, though, a jumped-up squirt. Nobody likes him, he knows it all. You know what I mean. There are rumours about his wife, though. She's supposed to be having an affair with the only non-clergy bloke living in the Close, one of those rented houses they've let to help the funds. A mass-market writer, would you believe it? Whispers, gossip, there might not even be any truth in the business but I'll tell you, if there is, then it'll liven the place up like it hasn't been livened up since Cromwell laid siege to it! Only time will tell."

Clay was silent; he was staring at that picture again as if those eyes hypnotised him. He was jerked out of his reverie by the clanging of the shop bell downstairs.

"A customer, a rare breed that I mustn't risk not even getting a glimpse of!" Drinkwater made for the stairs. "Nice to see you, Cecil. Drop by again sometime. I'm usually in most evenings after seven when choir practice has finished."

"I will, most certainly." Cecil Clay negotiated the steep staircase with care. He cast one last glance behind him; the girl in the picture was following his departure with her eyes, seeming to beg him to return.

And the thought that stuck in his mind was what somebody had done to Herbert Poppleton. He shuddered uncontrollably.

He almost lost his balance on the stairs, grabbed the rail with a sweating hand. Those eyes were still watching him, forcing him to meet their gaze. Their expression had changed; an icy trickle ran up his spine.

It was as if that unknown girl painted on a piece of wood was trying to tell him something.

Cecil Clay stumbled out into the street, grateful for the warmth of the sunshine and the milling crowd of tourists. Up above him, beyond the Minster Pool with its resident flotilla of quacking mallard, towered the spires of the cathedral.

Suddenly, for him, they took on a different meaning, no longer were they the bastion of his sheltered upbringing. They were sinister.

And, for no logical reason, threatening.

3

Sandra Corms had been bored and lonely for the last twelve years. Now, these last two months, all that had changed.

Rarely had she taken such trouble with her make-up, she hadn't needed to before. Her shoulder length dark hair was flecked with low lights; she smiled at herself in the mirror, stepped back to check her full-length reflection. Her phobia was being overweight; she had not bothered about that either until a few weeks ago. Maybe Weight Watchers had reduced her waistline, at least she was making an effort and she had cut down on chips and chocolate, her two devastating weaknesses. The green blouse and dark blue jeans fit snugly; she wasn't fat, she was big. And beautiful. That was what Gerald Norman kept telling her and she believed him. At 5ft 8in she had a large build that discreetly hid any surplus flesh.

Gerald's compliments nullified her husband's insults and sarcasm; nobody had ever paid her compliments like Gerald did repeatedly. And she knew he meant every word, even when he told her he was in love with her.

Having four children had not helped her figure. Julie was just twelve and was due to start 'big' school in the autumn. Sandra had become pregnant with Julie out of wedlock, otherwise she would not have married Michael; they were only dating casually at the time. Cathy was ten and Elaine was eight. One shouldn't have favourites amongst one's children, she told herself guiltily, but it was little Michael she felt for most. A break-up in her marriage would affect her seven-year-old son the most; he was her biggest tie to her dead marriage, the reason she wasn't ready to leave yet.

The children were all at school; she was going to have problems when the summer holidays arrived. Michael's parents always looked after them one day a week in the holidays to give her a break. Another pang of guilt; she would be exploiting her in-laws and that would be thrown in her face when everything came out. But her philosophy was to live for the day, and today she would do just that.

Michael asked for everything he got, her sister Louise had told her that. What other woman would stand for a weekly £80 housekeeping plus family allowance and her husband never gave her all of it together. Maybe £40 on a Monday, and then he would borrow fifteen back off her to go to the pub on Tuesday night. A tenner on Thursday and she might well still be owed the remaining £45 at the beginning of the next week. At least he paid for the dog food—that was one small consolation.

Michael went to the pub seven nights a week. He always had done so, right from the start of their hasty marriage. He had been assistant organist at the Cathedral for the last ten years, and it was his drinking which would deprive him of promotion. Not that alcohol ever affected his playing, he never drank in the daytime, but it was well known in the Close that the Shoulder of Mutton was his second home. Usually he stopped on in the Cathedral until 7.30 every evening, returned home for his meal and a change into casuals, and he was always out of the house by nine. He rarely came home before 11.30. He was never actually drunk, just nasty. Sandra usually feigned sleep; it was a more convincing excuse than the conventional headache one. Since Gerald, she hated Michael touching her.

Gerald was everything that Michael was not. He was kind and loving; his only regret was that he was unable to spend more time with her. Their illicit meetings revolved around Michael's absence, either at the pub or in the Cathedral, the children's schooling or out-of-school activities, and both had to coincide with Gerald's wife's absence from home. At times it was difficult synchronising all three. But they managed at least once a week.

There was a certain mystique about having an affair with a writer, Sandra thought. It wasn't like having a clerk or a shop assistant for a lover. Gerald was quite well known, both locally and nationally. His prolific output, over fifty novels published, some under pseudonyms, had earned him an enviable reputation in mass-market fiction. Mostly, he wrote thrillers. He was already working on the idea of giving her a secretarial job, a kind of PA. That way their meetings would become legitimate; it would overcome a lot of problems.

Sandra kept asking herself 'Why me?' Gerald had already told her why; his reasons were so flattering that she hardly believed them. All right, she was big and beautiful; he had just about convinced her of that. Kind and considerate; she had not thought of herself that way. Loving; she was in love with him all right. It had taken her weeks to tell him, she had only told Michael that once in twelve years of marriage and then she had lied.

Gerald's wife was a hard one; she had virtually driven her husband into Sandra's arms. Greedy, unfeeling, spent a lot of time out on her own social activities. She was almost the female equivalent of Michael; Sandra laughed aloud at the thought.

She checked her watch. It was 10.30 on a bright summer's morning. Michael had accompanied Frame, the organist, to a seminar in Birmingham. Jane Norman had gone on a Women's Institute coach trip to Bath. The children were at school. Sandra didn't have to pick them up until three thirty. Which reminded her, there was a slow puncture in one of the tyres on the VW estate; Michael had procrastinated about taking it to the garage to get it fixed. In case it needed a new tyre.

She let herself out of the house. It was going to be a lovely day, the loveliest day of her life.

* * * * *

Rupert Frame was uneasy. He had not used to feel nervous about staying on late in the Cathedral, long after the doors were closed to the public. But he was tonight and he knew why. He had read the report of the inquest into Herbert

Poppleton's death. There had been a lengthy piece in *The Telegraph* that morning. It made for grisly reading.

"*Genital amputation leading to death by loss of blood. Murder by person or persons unknown.*"

The police were following up on a number of leads; they were still looking for the driver of a red Ford Focus seen in the vicinity of the Malvern Hills on the day of Poppleton's killing.

They wouldn't find him, Frame was sure of that. The psychopath would strike again. Because he was sick and he didn't need a reason to kill.

The nape of Rupert Frame's neck tingled. A nagging sensation, a feeling that he was being *watched*. That was stupid; there was nobody in the tranquil gloom of the Cathedral on a late summer evening to watch him. The Verger on late duty – it was Needes this week – had locked the door behind him, gone for his evening meal. He was due back at nine; it was only 8.30 and Needes was one of those who would not work ten minutes more than was absolutely necessary.

Frame stood up, stretched his gaunt body, peered over the balcony of the organ loft. Discreet lighting showed him the presbytery, empty choir stalls. He glanced down at the nave, tried to see behind the pillars into the north and south aisles, but it was too dark. Shadows took on shapes, moved and were still again, blended back into the blackness. There was nothing there, nothing untoward. Just tombs of long dead bishops. The sleeping children slept on. Nothing stirred.

Rupert Frame, your nerves are getting the better of you. You are over tired, working too many hours.

Here in the quiet of a deserted cathedral it did not sound convincing. Yet he sat down again. The Festival was only weeks away, there was much to be done. Scheduled services were innumerable; there were organ recitals and concerts, an exhausting workload. Only practice made perfect even when you were at the top of your job. He must give it another half hour, at least until Needes came to lock up.

His thoughts strayed. To his wife, Philippa. She was having a hard time of it, they both were, because of Adrian. Their teenage son was an embarrassment to them, to the Close. Only last week he had been in trouble with the police again, a fight in Breadmarket Street. Adrian had not been drinking, that was one vice he left alone. Twice he had been prosecuted for being in possession of cannabis. A lot of youths today used the drug, but that didn't excuse him. Adrian had a problem that went deeper than drugs, a psychiatric one, but nobody seemed able or willing to treat him for it. Rupert and Philippa had tried everything they could think of, every source available to them; psychiatrists fobbed them off, doctors were unsympathetic. So was the Dean. Rupert's job could be on the line.

He tried to play, missed a note, but it did not matter tonight, because there was nobody to listen to him.

Was there?

A cathedral was a good place for a psycho on the run to hide, far safer and much more comfortable than sleeping in subways.

Rupert missed another note.

He didn't have to stay late, he made his own work schedule, he was answerable only to his conscience. If he was gone when Needes came back, it was no business of the Verger's.

Go home, whilst you still can.

There was tomorrow night, and the night after. Weeks of nights during which the hidden watcher could observe him. Except that there was nobody there, never had been.

There was.

Something moved down there, a noise like a footstep that echoed in the silence. Just one.

Frame tensed, felt the sweat trickling down his brow. He began to tremble and remembered again what had happened to Poppleton. But that had been a long way from here; there could not possibly be any connection with the

Cathedral. The other just happened to have been an organist here once. That was the only link.

A stifled cough, it was magnified in the stillness, eerie like the whispers of tourists when they crept down the aisles whilst a service was in progress.

"Who's there?" Rupert intended it to sound authoritative, stern and demanding, but the question came out quivering, the high recesses of the building picked it up, repeated it.

Who's … there … there … there?

Nobody answered. Neither footfall nor cough. The silence surged softly back.

Rupert walked nervously, shakily, along the balcony, began to descend. He would leave. Now. This minute. Walk purposefully looking neither to the right nor the left. Nor behind. The way one walked late at night in an alien city, determined not to hesitate, not to catch the eye of a loiterer and invite trouble.

He would be able to open the north door from the inside; he would leave it for Needes to lock. The Verger surely would not be long now. Maybe he should warn him. No, it was illogical; in all probability the noise had been made by something falling, a prayer book toppling from one of the pews because it has been left precariously balanced.

But prayer books did not cough.

Frame's footsteps hollowed on the floor, sounded like mocking laughter pursuing him. He fought the urge to run. It was only a matter of yards to the north transept.

His heart was hammering, his temples throbbed. His legs felt as though they would crumple under him at any second, tumble him to the floor. Unable to get up again, lying there in the darkness, waiting for …

"I hope I didn't startle you, sir."

Rupert jumped, almost lost his balance as he whirled round; there was a scream loaded into his throat in readiness. His arms went up as if to ward off a sudden blow from a crazed attacker, instinctively protecting his head.

He doesn't go for the head. Remember what he did to poor old Herbert?

"Who is it?" Another whisper for the echoes, a quiver of fear.

"I'm sorry, I didn't mean to scare you, sir."

A shape that was denser than the surrounding shadows stood up against a stone pillar. A silhouette that was powerfully built, smooth where the head balded. Eyes that seemed to glow malevolently in the darkness.

"Homer!" Frame spat the name out in mingled relief and anger.

"I'm sorry, sir." A mocking apology. Because I meant to scare the hell out of you.

"It's all right." Rupert fought to get himself under control, waited for his nerves to steady so that when he spoke again it would not be another trembling croak.

Damn the fellow, he was always creeping around the place like a ghoul, seemed to glide rather than walk.

Charles Homer was in his late seventies, had started here straight from school, worked his way up to Head Verger by stepping into dead men's shoes. He had been here in Poppleton's time. Now why the devil did Herbert have to come into it again?

Homer's skin had dried and withered over the years, seemed to be stretched over his skull. His dried cracked lips parted occasionally in a mirthless smile.

Eyes that never left you, you had the impression that they never blinked, made you uneasy. Scared you. Like now.

His dark suit and gown rendered him almost invisible against the background shadows, gave an illusion of a bodiless skull floating in the air. Once his body had been powerful; he claimed to hold a black belt. But he was a romanticiser, a bragger, if you lingered long enough to let him talk.

There were rumours, too, about him. Frame had heard them from Canon Feiffer, the Precentor, and you could not always believe what he told you. Feiffer and Homer had a long established feud that went back thirty years, a trivial row that had never been allowed to die. Frame wasn't interested in petty quarrels; the Close was long overdue a new generation.

"I thought Needes was on late duty, Homer?" A veiled reprimand. What the hell are you doing creeping around in here when you should be off duty?

"He is, sir." Those fixed eyes never flinched, there was defiance in them. "But I always keep a check on my men." And on you.

"That's what I call devotion to duty." The intended sarcasm didn't come over; it was an unintended compliment.

"Thank you, sir."

"I'm leaving now, Homer."

"I thought I should check that you are all right, sir, in here on your own at night." Homer had an obsession with security and his greatest concern – which he widely publicised – was that the priceless Lichfield Gospels, now permanently on show in the Chapter House, might be either damaged by vandals or stolen.

"And why should I not be all right, Homer?" What a damn fool question to ask; Frame knew what the reply would be.

"Well, you know what happened to Mr Poppleton, sir." The expression was stoic, not so much as a flinch of those eyes, no hint of mockery. A kind of threat voiced without emotion. "Somebody did a terrible thing to him and they haven't caught the fellow yet. Who knows, he might be hiding out in here somewhere."

Rupert Frame hurried from the Cathedral. He was a very frightened man.

4

Canon Feiffer sat typing in the bow window of his red-bricked house, which faced the north side of the Cathedral. He hammered the keys of the pre-1960s Royal machine with two meaty fingers, using such force that both carbon copies showed signs of perforation. He believed in forthrightness, both with the spoken word and the written word, strength of character. No modern typewriter would have withstood decades of such determined physical abuse.

He pulled the paper from beneath the roller, spread it out and checked his work, made a minor correction with a fountain pen. His glasses were pushed up on to his wide forehead; his puffed cheeks reflected the anger in his letter. How dare those impudent schoolboys focus a pair of binoculars on his wife's bedroom window! Doubtless they were hoping to glimpse Mrs Feiffer partly unclothed, lusting after her bared flesh. Well, they would most certainly have been disappointed for the only place where she stripped completely was in the bathroom and that had an opaque glass window. Thank goodness! But that wasn't the point, most certainly it was not. Their intention had been to look upon an unsuspecting naked lady of irreproachable morals, a God-fearing woman whom no man other than himself had viewed in a state of undress. That was unforgivable in his eyes and in God's.

He was reminded of poor old Herbert Poppleton's boast of never having seen Maude naked in fifty years of marriage. All credit to them both for their self-control; it most certainly had not impaired their relationship. Canon Feiffer could not claim such abstention for either himself or his wife, certainly not in their early marital years. May had been a comely girl then; since middle age, she had put on an awful lot of weight. That had not, he told himself repeatedly, anything to do with them sleeping in separate bedrooms; he was an asthmatic, he snored loudly, and a double room would not have been fair to his dear wife.

Those boys must be disciplined. He ran his shaking fingers through his thinning grey hair, they came away slippery with perspiration. Had Wilson still been Headmaster, then the matter would have been settled irrevocably in that fine man's own inimitable manner. Six of the best for all concerned, their bottoms would have stung for days, and the offending binoculars would have been confiscated and consigned to the dustbin.

Charlesworth, the current headmaster, was not in the same mould; he lacked strength of character. He never used the cane; his excuse was that corporal punishment had been abolished. Poppycock! The Cathedral School was no namby-pamby state institution; it was an establishment that prepared boys, mentally and physically, for a God-fearing role in society. If you transgressed, you were punished harshly—it was the only way.

Wilson would not have pandered to any bureaucratic directive on how erring youth should learn the error of its ways. He would have caned regardless and the Dean and Chapter would have backed him. Some of them, like Feiffer himself, had been in office during Wilson's headmastership. They must make Charlesworth follow in the footsteps of a great man. Psychological codswallop amounted to nothing less than a let-off, a reprimand that in itself was often not stern enough and was forgotten in a short time. Don't waste time searching for reasons for misbehaviour—punish it swiftly.

Feiffer had pointed this out to Charlesworth in his letter. The headmaster must call an assembly, demand that the miscreants own up, and then cane them in front of the entire school. A public flogging.

Feiffer separated the copies, addressed two more envelopes. The Bishop and the Dean must be made aware of what had gone on. An accompanying letter urged both of his superiors to demand that the boys concerned were caned.

The precentor's eyesight had not been good enough to identify the voyeurs. That did not matter, they would doubtless confess. If they remained guiltily silent, then the whole school must be punished, perhaps a forfeiture of leisure time, a weekend long detention. Or a suspension of parental visits.

He wrote to Charlesworth, whereas, years ago, he would have demanded a personal audience with Prebendary Wilson. Because he detested talking to the younger man, listening to nonsensical theories about how modern youth needed to express themselves and the older generation must be tolerant of their misdeeds. There would be some piffling excuse, a lie; there were starlings nesting in the crumbling chimney pot, that was all the boys were looking at, Canon Feiffer had jumped to hasty conclusions, fourteen-year-old pupils were not interested in peeping on a female in her seventy-ninth year.

Well, Charlesworth would have the complaint in writing; the Bishop and the Dean would have copies of the letter. Correspondence was never ignored; it was a strict diocesan rule. The matter would have to be investigated, the truth would come out. It just remained to be seen what action would be taken.

Canon Feiffer licked the adhesive on the envelopes, stuck the flaps down, thumped them with his fist to ensure they did not unfurl. Stationery was no longer of the high quality of the past. He banged on the stamps with his fist as an added precaution.

He stood up, prepared to embark upon one of his many daily shambling walks down to the post box at the bottom of the Close.

The Close was crowded with tourists; they had probably come by coach, he noted some American accents. He scowled in their direction, cleared his throat loudly, disapprovingly. Some cars were parked by the shop and cafe; he hoped that their owners were residents. The sooner wheel-clamping was introduced, the better. Visitors came to gawp at the architecture; they had no thought of its spiritual meaning. They were just sightseers; they had no *right* to be in this backwater of holy worship.

On the return trip he remembered that he needed to write to the Vicar Choral, this business with the voyeuristic boys had taken it right out of his mind. There was some urgency if a scandalous rumour was to be averted. It wasn't exactly a compliment, but somebody had mentioned to Feiffer that Drinkwater was having young visitors to his home in the evenings, voiced their disapproval. If you were a member of the Close, however slight your connection with the Cathedral, then you had to keep your nose clean; the vaguest suspicion about anything untoward was magnified out of all proportion.

Drinkwater was untidy—even wearing a suit he was scruffy, it just seemed to hang limply on his gaunt frame. Most likely the fellow did not even posses a trouser press. Suede shoes were not fitting to Choral duties, either; footwear should be black and highly polished—lace-ups, not slip-ons. And however he brushed his hair, *if* he brushed it, there were always unsightly tufts sticking up.

But that was not the nature of the canon's complaint. Yet. It was merely an addendum. The main reason for writing to the Vicar Choral was the rumours and there was no smoke without fire. Even if it was all perfectly innocent, it still *looked* bad. It had to stop.

Feiffer came to a decision as he re-entered his study. Perhaps it was the heat of the day, which dissuaded him from embarking upon another lengthy letter hammered out on that ancient keyboard. At eighty-two, correspondence was an irksome task; Bishop Franklyn employed a secretary to write *his* letters.

On this occasion, the precentor decided, he would speak to Drinkwater personally. It was a delicate matter, and was perhaps, on reflection, better not committed to paper. The written word was dangerous in this age of libel suits.

*****

Feiffer awaited his opportunity. He spent a lot of time observing the various movements in the Close from his window and he had formed an accurate mental timetable of choral routines. Evensong finished promptly at 5.15. Rupert Frame then took a break before returning at seven to rehearse for the festival programme. James Drinkwater slouched away to his garret over his bookshop in Dam Street. What on earth had the planning department been thinking of in allowing him to set up as a purveyor of lurid, immoral cheap fiction in such close proximity to the Cathedral? He probably had pornographic material hidden away in there too—he was the type. Shifty. Which added up to those rumours having a foundation for truth …

At 5.10 Feiffer stood in his porch, squinted in the direction of the west doors. His sight was not good enough to discern facial details but there was no mistaking the Vicar Choral's slovenly gait, the way he dragged his feet, had his hands thrust deep into his pockets.

The precentor lumbered forward, blew out his reddening cheeks, pursed his lips. He was very angry.

"Drinkwater!"

The other slowed, turned back almost arrogantly. There was no trace of respect in his expression as his gaze fell upon Canon Feiffer, just curiosity. Years ago, younger Chorals blanched when their names were called out.

"Yes, Precentor?"

"I'd like a word with you, Drinkwater. I think my study would be more appropriate than out here, don't you?" Feiffer had a slight impediment of speech, which resulted in a spray of spittle and a dribble of saliva when he was angry.

"As you wish." James Drinkwater shrugged, turned to follow the other. His hands remained in his pockets. He hoped that whatever the precentor wanted, it would not take too long. Cecil Clay was due to call round at six; they were eating out tonight. At McDonald's.

Feiffer seated himself in his leather armchair, deliberately did not offer his visitor a seat; that would have undermined his authority, reduced their meeting to a relaxed atmosphere. This way he held an advantage over the other.

"It has come to my ears," the precentor spoke slowly, giving the impression that he was either chewing on something or else enduring the discomfort of mouth ulcers, "that choirboys have been visiting you at your … er … accommodation. Names have even been mentioned … Sutcliffe, Colley, Pritchard-Williams. I have this information on reliable authority, Drinkwater."

"May I ask whose, sir?" Drinkwater stood with his hands clasped behind his back, respectful now but not humble. If the other's words were disconcerting, he showed no signs of guilt nor nervousness.

"You may not, Drinkwater." Feiffer was uneasy for a moment. His "information" had come from a conversation between Homer and Lumby, one of the new vergers. Homer had spoken in an unusually loud voice, almost as if it was his wish to be overheard, but that was unlikely because he could not possibly have known that Feiffer was browsing in the Cathedral Bookshop at the time, hidden from view by a rack of shelving. And if Homer had been aware of the precentor's presence nearby, then he most certainly would not have wished his conversation to be eavesdropped on by the precentor. So there had to be some truth in the gossip.

James Drinkwater lifted his head, met the other's hostile stare. His features were expressionless.

"Well, Drinkwater, do you admit or deny the allegation?"

"If you will excuse me saying so, sir," the Vicar Choral's voice was low, there was not a tremor in it, "I don't think there are grounds either for an admission nor a denial."

"Do you not?" The florid cheeks were distended, balloons that might burst if they were inflated further. "Well, *I* do!"

"The boys you mention *have* visited me." The "sir" was

dropped, but there was no outward sign of guilt or anger. The reply was almost casual.

"Do you realise the *implications* of such associations, Drinkwater?" The thick neck was thrust forward, a string of lengthening saliva swung from a thick lower lip like a spider descending from its web on a dewy morning.

"No, I do not. The boys you named, and Potter and Laines also, have visited me to talk over festival plans for choral productions. I believe that members of the choir should not be treated merely as voices, as they are by Mr Frame and Mr Corms. I require co-operation, teamwork, if I am to get the best out of the choir. It is imperative to strike up a *working* relationship in order to achieve this. I think that I have done just that, Precentor."

"I don't like it." Feiffer sprayed spittle, thumped his knee. "And the Dean and Chapter will like it even less if word reaches them, I can assure you of that. Choirboys visiting Vicar Chorals smacks of an unhealthy association. It also fuels rumours that are damaging to the Church."

"I disagree."

"Do you?" Feiffer sat upright, his head was thrust forward, a vein throbbed in his forehead. Rarely had he had anybody disagree with him before.

"Herbert Poppleton had members of the choir visit him at his house on a regular basis for years." Drinkwater spoke evenly; there was no trace of dissent in his tone.

"Oh, did he?" The other was visibly taken aback. "And how do you know that, Drinkwater?"

"Because I was one of his choirboys, sir."

"I see." Feiffer closed his eyes momentarily, then opened them again and added belligerently, "But Herbert Poppleton was *married,* Drinkwater."

"Does that make a difference, sir?"

"I'm afraid so." The precentor had averted his eyes; he seemed embarrassed. "God made man and then he made woman so that they might live together and procreate."

"His wife was never there, sir, when I visited. She left tea and scones on the table. I think she went for a rest upstairs. Whatever the cause, she was never around. You *must* have known about that, Precentor?"

Feiffer did not reply. His puffed out cheeks drained of their colour, and when finally he spoke his voice was almost a whisper. "Herbert Poppleton was the *organist*, Drinkwater."

"Does that place him above suspicion, gossip, and rumours?"

"There were none."

"None that you heard."

Canon Feiffer crossed one leg over the other. The fingers, which lowered his glasses back down on to the bridge of his nose, shook a little. "I merely mention it, Drinkwater, in case … in case people should start talking."

"Thank you, sir, I appreciate it. I will bear it in mind."

"Doubtless you know what happened to poor Herbert Poppleton, a tragedy which has shaken the Close to the core."

"I hardly think that has any bearing upon the matter which you mentioned, Precentor."

"No, no, of course not. But, please remember, you are a Vicar Choral, not an organist. Nor assistant organist. Mr Frame, I am sure, does not invite boys round to his home. I would advise you to be more discreet, Drinkwater."

"Thank you, sir."

"That is all."

Canon Feiffer turned back to his desk, left his visitor to depart alone. The precentor experienced a sense of anticlimax. Defeat, almost. The meeting, for once, had not gone according to plan; the admonishment, which he had rehearsed in his mind, had backfired.

His jumbled thoughts switched to Herbert Poppleton, and for once he was uneasy. He had known that choirboys had visited the organist, but that was years ago. And even if Maude had been upstairs, she had been in the house. So that made it all right. Because Herbert was beyond reproach, a legend in his own time. None questioned his actions.

All the same, he had been horribly murdered, mutilated, and his killer was still at large.

5

"Let's make a cuppa." Sandra attempted to straighten her dishevelled hair as she dressed.

"If you like." Gerald Norman still lay on the bed, a sheet draped over his naked body as though he was suddenly inhibited. His eyes watched her closely as if he was afraid that it was all a dream, that she might suddenly disappear and he would awake to reality after a pleasant siesta. He reached out a hand to touch her, just to make sure.

"Oooh!" she giggled. "You made me jump, Gerry."

"Give us a kiss, then." He pulled her back so that she lay across him.

Their lips met, their eyes closed.

"Funny thing, I don't feel guilty anymore." For once, she was serious.

"You used to feel guilty?"

"Didn't you?"

"In a way." He stroked his short clipped dark beard meditatively. "But not like you. You see, it's different for me—my marriage was on the rocks years ago, we've only really held together until the kids were old enough to go their own way. Jane's been going hers for a long time."

"Like WI outings?"

"Aren't you ever serious?" He raised his eyes heavenwards.

"Seldom."

"That's what I like about you." He kissed her again. "Life's been just too serious, I could grow old young."

"Like fifty-three."

"All right, rub it in. You're twenty-three years younger than me."

"And nobody would ever guess," she laughed, afraid that she had offended him. "Gerry, anybody who didn't know would take you for forty."

"Thanks."

"My pleasure." She pulled back the sheet, looked down on him. He had looked after his body, all right, kept himself fit. Maybe his legs were too thin, but what the hell. He wanted to be young, he thought young. So he was young.

"Finished?"

"I'll go downstairs and put the kettle on. I'll have to be away by three today."

"Quarter of an hour earlier than usual? You don't have to pick the kids up until 3.30 and it's less than ten minutes' drive."

"I … I bumped the car yesterday. Or, rather, somebody else did. So I have to walk down today to collect the kids."

"Oh Christ!"

"Nothing too bad. That bloody woman Fiona, you know she always reverses down to the bottom of the Close instead of going all the way round like the rest of us do. Well, I was just turning in from going to the chippie, and *bang*, she'd hit me. I'll need a new bonnet, wing, headlight and bumper. I got an estimate for it, nearly three grand!"

"Jesus!" Gerry pursed his lips.

"Michael says the insurance will write it off, probably give us two and a half grand. He reckons he can buy it back cheap off them, get a good knock-out job done for around a grand."

"And he'll pocket the profit for himself!" Gerry's lips curled with contempt. "Big Ears doesn't miss a trick! Don't forget, you put eleven hundred towards the car initially from that policy you had mature. So in effect, Mike's pocketing your money and giving you a banged out banger to ride round in."

"He'll never change." She stood up, smoothed her hands down her jeans. "I'll go put that kettle on."

"Things will change." He smiled at her. "For the better. I promise you that."

"I believe you." She stooped down and their lips brushed again. "I love you, Gerry."

"And I love you." He let her go this time, looked around for his scattered clothes. Life was really good right now.

* * * * *

"I still can't believe it." Sandra stared down at her tea. "Two months ago we met for the first time and I almost chickened out of meeting you at the Lion that day."

"And then you proceeded to tell me that it was better to stop it all before it started. So you went on holiday feeling miserable and I moped here at home, struggled to work. Then you phoned me and it was all on again. Crazy!"

"Something you said." Her hand found his. "You said, 'Fate decreed that we met, we can't throw it all away.' After you'd gone, I realised that you were right, and I almost burst into tears."

"Well, we got together and that's all that matters." He squeezed her hand. "I'll phone you tonight."

"No, I'll phone you first, just to be on the safe side. You can always count on Michael being out of the house by 10.15, but it'd be awkward if he answered the phone. I'll phone you, then you can ring me back. I don't want his phone bill clocking up, he might start asking for an itemised statement and then the shit would hit the fan."

"Would you worry if it did?"

"Not really, but I'd rather it didn't just yet."

"How long have I got to wait?"

"Four years."

"You keep saying that, I was hoping we could make it sooner."

"Maybe." She seemed uncertain of herself, her eyes misted. "I'd like to go now, but I'd like to see little Michael at big school first. It's him I'm worried about most. One shouldn't have favourites, but …"

"I know." He nodded. "But maybe we can work something out."

"Maybe," she said unconvincingly.

"We will. Somehow."

"It's all so unbelievable." She pulled him close to her. "I can't get used to the idea of being with a writer."

"You've been married to an organist for twelve years. One makes music, the other makes words."

"*Assistant* organist," she corrected him, laughed.

"You have to be a special breed to live with a writer; they have one of the highest marriage casualty rates. Money isn't regular; sometimes it doesn't come at all. Trying to sell a book can be heart breaking."

"You haven't done so badly yourself, Gerry."

"No-oo." He pulled a pipe from his pocket, flicked his lighter, and enveloped them both in a cloud of aromatic smoke. "But times aren't good. And I'm a hack."

"What's that?"

"I write anything I can for money. I've got a good track record, and that's why nobody will take me seriously. I want to write the Big One, but convincing publishers that it's anything different from what has gone before is almost impossible. I won't rest until I've done it, though. Jane never had faith in me in that respect; she didn't want me to speculate on a lot of work that might all come to nothing."

"I'm with you all the way."

"Thank you." His voice was suddenly husky. "I'd like to make a start sooner than four years hence, though."

"I'd like that, too, Gerry."

"Ring me tonight." He held her hand all the way to the door.

"Michael's edgy," she said suddenly.

"You think he's suspicious?"

"Not Michael, it'll be the biggest shock of his life when it all comes out. No, I'm sure he doesn't suspect anything. He doesn't say a lot, but I think Frame, the organist, is getting him down. The guy's a neurotic lately, according to Michael. Nervy, jumpy, snaps at you over the slightest thing. I guess he's uptight over the Festival; they've got organ recitals and extra services. Frame goes back to the Cathedral on his own rehearsing most nights. He's tried to persuade Michael to go with him but you know Michael, he won't miss a night at the pub. It's all got very boring over the last twelve years."

"The winds of change are beginning to blow." Gerry kissed her before she stepped outside. "I get the feeling that an awful lot is going to happen, maybe sooner than we think."

As she turned away, Sandra's flesh goose pimpled. It was as though an icy hand was stroking her spine right the way up to her neck. Suddenly, she was very frightened and she did not know why. Not because of herself and Gerry; it was like a premonition that she did not understand.

6

"If you don't start relaxing, you'll go and have a heart attack before Festival week even starts!"

Philippa Frame played nervously with her fingers, stared at them as if they were the most important thing in the world to her right now.

"I'm all right, I tell you." Rupert Frame's tone was irritable, and he spread his *Telegraph,* held it up so that it hid his expression, but there was no disguising the fact his hands shook.

"You don't *need* to rehearse every night, surely?"

"Every musician needs to practise daily!" he snapped irritably, rustled his newspaper. "You should know that by now."

"I think you're becoming obsessive." Philippa began clearing the table. "That's what worries me most."

"Rubbish."

"Michael Corms doesn't go back to the Cathedral in the evenings unless there's a special reason for doing so."

"Corms will never make anything of himself. He's got the talent, but he won't use it any more than he has to. He's lazy and has a drink problem. Everybody knows that he's in the pub seven nights a week, but nobody will speak to him about it. Canon Feiffer's been having a mental about the boys from the school focusing binoculars on his wife's bedroom window, but he hasn't said a word about Michael's boozing. He always gets his priorities wrong. I guarantee that if Poppleton had still been organist, Michael Corms would either have gone teetotal or else been kicked out of the job. Like you say, dear, everybody is aware that Corms is drinking himself to death, but nobody has the guts to tell him."

"Why don't you tell him, then, Rupert?"

Frame lowered his paper and Philippa saw how drawn his gaunt features were, pouches beneath his eyes; he looked mentally and physically drained. "I intend to." He spoke softly, almost regretfully. "*After* the Festival. I can't risk him walking out before, there would be no time to appoint another assistant, let alone expect him to learn all the pieces in time. So I have to pander to Corms, it goes against the grain."

"I've heard something else." Philippa whispered, as if she feared there might be an eavesdropper, or possibly because she felt guilty about repeating gossip she had heard in the coffee shop.

"About Corms? That he's got a fancy woman? That wouldn't surprise me, Pip."

"No, not about him, about his wife. She's having it off with Norman. You know, the so-called writer." A hint of contempt for one who made his living out of lurid fiction whilst Rupert struggled to provide for his family on classical music. Everybody, it seemed, had got their priorities wrong, there was no justice either in the Close or in the world at large.

"Oh, I see." Disappointment because it wasn't Michael Corms. "I hardly know the woman; she never comes to the Cathedral."

"She's got to be a slut." Philippa crumpled the dishcloth up into a ball. "Mind you, Norman shouldn't be living in the Close, he's nothing to do with the Cathedral."

"I guess the Dean and Chapter are only too pleased to let any empty property to anybody these days," Frame leaned back in his chair, let his eyelids droop. "They must've vetted him but obviously not deeply enough. When they knew he was a writer, that was fine. Who more fitting than a literary gentleman in a city with a history of great writers and which now holds its own literary prize competition? They just omitted to find out what he wrote. What you say doesn't surprise me, Pip. All hell will be let loose when the news gets out, if it hasn't already done so. I've little sympathy for Michael; he probably drove her to another man by stopping out at the pub half the night, every night.

But he'll lose his job, you mark my words. The Church won't stand for scandal."

"Mind you, I'm not saying it's true," she spoke quickly, regretting perhaps that she had told her husband. "Mrs Craig had heard it in the Arts Centre cafe—it was she who told me. It could be guesswork, somebody putting two and two together and making five. I don't want you to repeat it. You won't, will you, Rupert?"

"Of course not." He smiled reassuringly. "There's a lot of unfounded gossip going around at the moment. I hear that Feiffer has carpeted Drinkwater for inviting choirboys round to his place. Again, there's probably nothing in it, but highlighting it sows the seeds of suspicion."

"Drinkwater's not married." Philippa turned back from the draining board. "And he's pally with that Clay chap, and he's as queer as a nine-bob note."

"You don't even know that, Pip." Her husband wagged a finger. "You women get together and presume too much. Some men are loners without being gay. Introverts, recluses who have relied upon their parents throughout life, and when the parents die they just go into a cocoon."

"Well, Clay bought a nude picture from the exhibition in the Arts Centre." Philippa was defensive, annoyed that her husband did not agree with her. "Under very suspicious circumstances."

"You mean he walked in there, made sure that nobody was looking, and tucked it under his raincoat. Then he surreptitiously slipped the supervisor a handful of notes on the way out?"

"You're being flippant," she snapped. "No, not quite like that, but he phoned up one morning, said he'd like to buy the painting and would they have it wrapped up for him to collect."

"A lot of people would do that, even for a still life painting."

"Except that he slunk into the gallery, pretended to be viewing the exhibition until the place was empty, and then he made a beeline for the desk, his cheque already made out, grabbed the parcel, and virtually ran out into the street. Apparently, so Miss Jeavons tells me, his face was as red as a beetroot."

"He probably just collects artwork." Frame returned to his newspaper. "Just as Corms's wife might have a legitimate reason for calling on friend Norman. Perhaps she's doing secretarial work for him. You ladies have got too much time on your hands and you've got dirty minds."

"You're impossible, Rupert."

"Maybe. Where's Adrian?"

"I'm not sure." Her voice trembled. "Somewhere in town with his mates, I guess. Smoking pot or getting drunk with Michael Corms. Or starting a fight. Doubtless the police will give us an update on his movements. Oh, Rupert, if only you'd spend more time with Adrian instead of with Bach and Mendelssohn."

"Teenagers don't want their father hanging around with them."

"Young boys do. That's the root of Adrian's trouble, Rupert, he never had a father because you were always practising or rehearsing or whatever. That's why he's like he is now!" Her voice rose to a shrill crescendo.

"Perhaps now you can see why I don't stay at home more." Rupert Frame rose to his feet, tossed his paper to one side. "Maybe it's the same for Michael Corms—who knows? I'm going to the Cathedral, I'll see you later."

"I'll be asleep in bed," she called after him. "And I wouldn't miss you if you never came home!"

Which, Rupert Frame thought as he let himself out of the front door, was not a nice thing for a wife to say to her husband. Suppose he had a sudden heart attack and dropped dead? She would regret those words for the rest of her life.

But he wasn't going to have a heart attack. The Festival was getting closer daily, they could not manage without him. Nevertheless, he experienced a twinge of guilt; Philippa was right, he had not been the best of fathers to their wayward son.

* * * * *

Rupert Frame was far from happy with his performance. Even in a locked and empty cathedral, his main critic was present. Himself. And he was a perfectionist.

Tonight he could not seem to get into the necessary mood. He had struggled for over an hour with Messiaen's set of nine meditations of *La Nativité du Seigneur.* They eluded him, his mood failed to harmonise with them.

He took a breather, leaned on the balcony looking down the nave towards the west doors. Rows of pews, in the shadows one could almost imagine that they were filled with a discerning audience. Not a congregation; there was a difference. Faceless forms that sat in silence, did not applaud his performance, because that was forbidden in the Cathedral. Heads that should have nodded their approval remained motionless.

You are stupid, he told himself, *there is nobody out there. Just shadows. And tombs and monuments to the long dead.*

Everybody here except himself was dead.

He was edgy. Frightened. Each night the fear came to plague him, but still he came back here.

There was nobody there except the dead.

He took a deep breath, thought that he might be getting one of his rare asthma attacks. If so, it would pass, they were only mild. A kind of shallow breathing when you fought to fill your lungs. It was stuffy in here.

He tried to remember whom the duty Verger was tonight. He did not think it was Needes; it was probably Lumby. Lumby was a likeable fool; not very intelligent, but he managed to do the job. A big man, overweight, always smiling with a set of buck teeth. Your classic fool: if there was anything to trip over, Lumby would fall over it. He tried to balance a pile of hymn books, tiptoed with gargantuan steps that echoed throughout this vast place, dropped the lot with a clatter. Homer chided him, bullied him, but Lumby still grinned.

Rupert was sure that Lumby was on night duty; if he really wanted to know, he only had to walk down to the desk by the west doors and check the roster in Homer's notebook. But it didn't really matter.

Because the organist was afraid to walk down the aisle with all those people watching him. Even if they weren't there, he did not want to draw attention to himself.

You're not a proper father, Rupert. You neglected your son when he needed you most. Shut up, Pip, you're the last person I need here.

He returned to the organ, consulted his watch by the small strip light. 9.45. He wasn't going home yet. Why should he? Michael Corms would be getting steadily drunk whilst his wife was being unfaithful to him. Drinkwater would be entertaining choirboys in his dowdy flat. Clay would be gazing lustfully upon his nude painting; why didn't he save himself the money and go buy a soft porn mag from the top shelf in the newsagents? And Feiffer would be busy writing letters of complaint to the Dean and Chapter and walking down to the bottom of the Close to post them.

Adrian would probably be in custody on a drugs, drink or assault charge. Which was yet another reason for not going home.

And what was Philippa doing? Rupert had never given much thought to what she did whilst he was out. It was intriguing because he didn't really know what she did in the evenings. She might even be having an affair, like Corms's wife.

The organist almost burst into laughter at the idea. Oh Jesus, I'd love to see her, to see if she had the guts to go with another man. Her sharp mouth shaping up for a kiss, her sagging breasts being fondled, her straight legs with their thick ankles stretched wide. She's probably still got her ankle socks on; she kept a pair to wear in bed on winter nights.

The crazy vision came and went; he found he could

breathe easier afterwards. Light relief, the relaxing of tension. He would not have minded if she had a lover because it might have made her normal. *It's your fault that Adrian's like he is, Pip, not mine. Because you were always trying to make him something he wasn't. You're a hypocrite.*

I'm what I am, and nothing will change that, I'm married to my organ, I'll stay with it all night if I want. Yes, I'll have an affair with it.

You've been having an affair with it for years, Rupert. Like Herbert Poppleton did. And look what happened to him.

Rupert glanced along the balcony towards the top of the steps. There was nobody there. Or rather, it was too dark to see anybody if they were there.

He gave up on Messiaen. Bach was more suited to his present mood. He began to play *Toccata and Fugue in D minor.*

That was better, decidedly better. He could almost find the mood. Almost, but not quite. He was too edgy.

He thought somebody coughed down below, but he could not be sure because the organ strains had not quite died away, lingered up in the roof. When they were finally gone, only silence remained. And that was worse.

"Is that you, Lumby?" A whisper that travelled down past the choir stalls and into the presbytery, faded away in the Lady Chapel.

There was no answer.

Lumby was slightly deaf, Rupert vaguely remembered. The other probably had not heard. Or it might be Homer creeping around like a ghoul again. The Head Verger would not reply—he would slink up the steps and onto the balcony, keep to the shadows. Then he would cough so that you jumped. *I'm sorry, sir, did I startle you?*

"Homer?"

Again, no answer. Rupert found himself listening for stealthy footfalls, but he heard none.

It was time to be going home. No, damn it, it wasn't. Corms would still be drinking, the assistant organist's wife would be fornicating, and Feiffer would be on his tenth letter of the evening. Adrian would be in a police cell. And Philippa *might* just be committing adultery.

Rupert didn't want to spoil *that.*

Somebody was coming up the steps to the organ loft.

Rupert heard them this time, he didn't imagine it. A scuffing of shoe leather, a rustle of loose clothing.

He wanted to shout out, 'Who's there? Is that you, Homer?' but the words would not come. Inside his head, *La Nativité du Seigneur* suddenly came right and he wondered why he had had trouble with it before.

There was a shape on the balcony that looked vaguely like a man. It might have been a carved statue that had moved out of place; in the deep gloom it could have been anything or nothing.

Frame froze at the organ. His hands wanted to play; his legs were suddenly too weak to run. He asked again if it was Homer, but the question remained inside his head, the words jammed in his throat. He could smell his own sweat.

Whoever it was moved closer, seemed to shuffle, always keeping to the shadows. An indeterminable shape: if it was tall, it stooped; if it was short, it stretched up, stood on the balls of its feet. Faceless, sexless, a being that might not even have been human.

Now it was within reach, but it did not stretch out a hand. It just stood there watching. If it had eyes with which to see.

"It is you, isn't it, Homer?" The words came out at last, belated and shaking.

Of course it was Homer. It had to be; it could not be anybody else. Homer was always creeping about the Cathedral, watching. Coughing meaningfully.

The other cleared his throat.

"I'm just leaving, Homer. I'm going home this very minute." *Just in case you think I'm staying.*

Rupert Frame stood up. His legs almost crumpled under him, he had to hold on to the organ for support. He felt suddenly faint; fear and the constriction of the blood in his legs caused him to lose his balance. He fell backwards, sat on the organ, thighs wide and defenceless.

A sudden rush of piped music, an expellation that might have been Messiaen or Bach being released in a tuneless roar that drowned his screams as the knife blade plunged deep into his soft flesh.

The attacker gouged and slashed until he was finished. Then, almost lovingly, he cleaned the bloodied blade on a strip of torn trouser and calmly retraced his steps down below.

His footsteps echoed as he walked towards the north transept and let himself out into the balmy night.

7

Ford had long learned by experience that one should let a case like this roll. In the early stages you went with the flow, let routine procedures take their course. You kept an open mind, did not jump to conclusions. You didn't try to tell anybody how to do their job even if you thought they were doing it wrong; you kept your eyes and ears open and your mouth shut. If you had any hunches, you shelved them, played them later when the dust had settled.

Detective Sergeant Jason Ford always had the feeling that he was a marked man with the CID, something that might have bordered on a persecution complex if he had not kept it under control. He would always be remembered as an ex-vice squad man, his sideways move to the CID security regarded as a demotion. Because he had not 'made it,' he'd had his ass kicked out all the way down to Rykneld Street. Because you never got credit below the rank of Chief Inspector; that had been Ford's mistake, he had, and still was, paying the price for it.

That had been back in the days when Dawson was Chief of Vice. Ford had trusted Dawson—another mistake. When you played a gut feeling, closed the rulebook, you put everything on the line. If you were wrong, they used you as a scapegoat. If you were right … Dawson had still used him, moved him to save embarrassment. The credit went to the department, the top man.

"You'd better work on the Frame case." Detective Chief Inspector Borman handed Ford a file. "Privately, we're linking it to the Poppleton murder, but that's confidential at the moment."

Jason Ford nodded. He detected an echo of Detective Chief Superintendent Anson's Directive: Borman was only one more in the pecking order. It was widely rumoured that the chief inspector had his sights on the top job, which made him a dangerous man when you were subordinate to him.

Ford flicked through the file; there was a day's reading here. All routine, but you had to ensure that you did not waste time going over ground already covered. A list of interviews already conducted; all negative.

"Take it and study it, Sergeant. Don't waste time browsing it here."

Ford was small and stocky, his ruddy complexion added to his lived-in features; aggressive if the need arose, a man of few words otherwise. His eyes never revealed his thoughts. His dark hair was cropped short and at 39 it was difficult to guess his age accurately, give or take five years either way.

His dedication to duty had not lessened even after the Black Mantis case when Dawson had had him transferred to CID; they could have put him back in uniform. At least he'd got a wife out of that investigation: WPC Brenda Braithwaite. Things might have been different without her. Now she was out of the force and he was still in it. He was not one to dwell on the past, what might or might not have been.

"I'll crack on," he stood up, met Borman's gaze and held it until the other averted his eyes.

"Best of luck, Sergeant." For us, not for you. "I'll leave it to you how you tackle it." So that we have somebody to blame if anything goes wrong.

"I'll start at the roots." Ford's voice was low, scarcely audible. *In case you think I've gone to Malvern for the bracing air and the spa water.*

"Up to you." Borman returned to a bulky file on his desk, only putting on his glasses after the door had closed behind Ford.

* * * * *

It was scorching hot in Malvern. Like it was everywhere else this summer. Which might have induced lethargy in anybody else but Jason Ford.

He checked with Inspector Coleorton, it was only courtesy when you were off your own patch; Poppleton was Malvern's pigeon, but he could be Lichfield's, too.

Ford had no trouble finding the murder scene; there were a group of sightseers there, a family of two generations and a loud-mouthed teenager who might have been the daughter's boyfriend. They had been poking about in the undergrowth, maybe looking for souvenirs. If there had been anything to find, Scene of Crime would have found it first. Ghouls came here most days; the mutilation had made the front page of the tabloids.

"That's where they found the bugger." The youth slashed at some gorse with a stick he had broken off a tree. "Just there, I recognise it from the picture in the papers. Blimey, whoever did it has to be a sicko, he'd cut off the old boy's ..."

"Malcolm!" the auburn-haired girl interrupted him, glanced in the direction of her parents.

"I thought we were going on up to the Roman Camp." A tall, grey-haired man attempted to create a diversion.

"Yes, I'd like to go there," a woman with a squeaky voice added. "This place gives me the creeps. Oh, there's somebody else coming now. Why on earth anybody should want to see the place where a man was murdered beats me."

"Good afternoon." Ford gave a taciturn smile; he was not in the habit of engaging in idle banter with strangers. Except in the course of business. "I take it this is the place, then?"

"Too right it is!" There was a leer on the other's acne-covered features, his narrowed eyes sized up Ford. "But there's 'undreds bin 'ere before us, you only got to see 'ow the undergrowth's trampled down to know that. You won't find anything, we've already looked."

"*He* has," the older woman put in quickly.

"Wonder what they wanted to do that to an old guy for," Ford remarked casually. Everybody's opinion counted.

Sometimes, not very often, out of the mouths of thickos came forth inspiration.

"'E was an organist, weren't 'e?"

"I believe he was, now that you come to mention it."

"Played religious music and the like."

"I guess so."

"Well, that's why 'e was done, it's common sense, ain't it?"

"Because people don't like religious organ music?" Ford's eyebrows were raised. "I read that only two percent of the population go to church these days."

"The fanatics *all* go. They 'ave to. You take these foreigners with their musks, or whatever they call 'em. And if anybody offends 'em, then they put the sentence of death on 'im and the poor guy goes into hiding, in fear of 'is life."

"I see." Ford nodded with as much solemnity as he could muster. "Except that the murdered man was a Church of England organist, played in a cathedral."

"So what? The bigger you are, the more you offend. You take it from me, mister, 'e'd fell foul of someone, offended 'em. 'E thought 'e could 'ide away out 'ere in the country but they found 'im, did for 'im. I mean, it weren't no ordinary murder, was it? They cut 'is whatsit off to symbolise their own religion."

"Maybe they were eunuchs," Ford suggested.

"You-whats?"

"Never mind." Ford sauntered away. It was an interesting theory, far-fetched as it was. Every religion had its maniacs.

Ford had seen all he needed to see; the murder scene was firmly etched in his photographic memory. It might or might not serve a purpose, but he liked to know just where Herbert Poppleton had died.

* * * * *

"Did you get on with Mr Frame?"

Ford leaned on the railings by the Minster Pool, watched the ducks squabbling over a floating crust of soggy bread. He barely glanced at the boy by his side, fifteen-year-olds reacted in different ways to police questioning; you had to put them at their ease, gain their confidence. He could not have achieved that within the school precincts.

"He was all right so long as you did your best." Dick Pritchard-Williams screwed up his freckled face. "Muck about and he'd give you what for. He was neurotic, but I suppose that was because of his own son. Adrian was an embarrassment to his parents."

"I guess so." There was no point pretending that Ford did not know about Frame's son. "Do you think Adrian could have made enemies for his father? I mean, for example, introduced other boys to drugs and their parents hated his dad for bringing him into this world so that he could corrupt others?"

"I *suppose* it's possible. A bit far-fetched, don't you think, Mr Ford?"

"Exceedingly." Ford smiled. Sergeant Clifford had interviewed both Adrian and Frame's widow; Ford might need to talk to either or both of them at a later stage. But not just yet. "Did any of the choirboys dislike Mr Frame?"

"You mean … enough to kill him?"

"If you like."

"I don't think so. None of us really liked Frame, you'd never get close to him—he wasn't a guy you could talk to. Like I said, if you could sing and you didn't mess about in practices or in services, he was fine. He didn't have a sense of humour. Mostly, though, Mr Corms played at practice and Mr Drinkwater concentrated on training our voices."

"What about Corms?"

"He's fine, never causes any problems. He drinks a lot, you know. He goes to the pub every night."

Ford knew; he had already checked out Corms. He would talk to the assistant organist later. "And James Drinkwater?"

"He's a great guy once you get to know him. If you've got a problem, he'll help you. Most of us have been back to his place over the bookshop at various times. Then Canon Feiffer, the precentor, complained, thought single blokes ought not to invite boys home, and Mr Drinkwater said we'd have to cool it. One or two of us still pop in, though."

"What do you do there?"

"We chat, discuss various pieces. All very relaxed. I can't say I care for Mr Drinkwater's friend, though."

"Oh? Who's he?"

"His name's Cecil Clay, he's a right weirdo. I can't see why they're friendly except that they both deal in books. Clay usually makes an excuse to leave when any of us go there. I think he's embarrassed by young company. Both of them, Drinkwater and Clay, were in the choir themselves once, attended the school. Must've been back in the fifties.

"Probably why they're mates, reminisce over the good old days." Ford watched an aggressive mallard chasing the others away from the remnants of the soggy crust. "Both of them must've been in the choir when Poppleton was organist."

"They were. We talked about the murder. Both of them reckon it was a one-off, a psychopath just happened upon an old man out for a walk. A homosexual. After all, old women get raped and killed for kicks, don't they?"

"We live in a sick world," Ford said. "Killings without a motive are always the hardest to solve. Frame was practising for the Festival; somebody got into the cathedral, killed him and left. Lumby, the night Verger, had left the north transept unlocked in case Frame wanted to leave early whilst he popped down town for some fish and chips. And with the city packed with tourists, we're looking for the proverbial needle in a haystack. But, as the Dean and Chapter say, the Festival goes ahead and so do the recitals and services."

"Corms is taking over as organist for the Festival," Pritchard-Williams added. "It's a big task, I don't know whether he's up to it. He's nervous about it, I know. Did you know ... Oh, I guess, it doesn't matter, it's none of my business."

"Go on."

"Corms's missus is having an affair. Cormsey will go berserk when he finds out."

"Oh?" Ford stiffened. The old saying, "*Cherchez la femme*," had been the undoing of many a murderer in a crime of passion. "Who with?"

"A writer who rents a place in the Close. His name's Gerald Norman. I've seen Mrs Corms coming out of his house on more than one occasion so there has to be *something* in it."

"I see." The detective let out his pent-up breath. It was too much to hope for that Mrs Corms had been having an affair with Rupert Frame. "Well, it's all part of life's rich pattern. From what I read, most people are at it these days."

"Mr Ford?"

"Yes?"

"Do you think that … that the killer will strike again?"

"I wish I knew." Ford's laugh was nervous. "There's always a chance, I guess."

"Because that's what worrying Cormsey, you can tell. He can't wait to get out of the cathedral after practices and services, and he doesn't go back there to practise at night."

"Everybody's jittery." Ford turned away from the railings. "Thank you for your help, Dick. If I need to talk to you again, I'll be in touch."

Ford knew only too well that the only way they would catch the murderer was if he struck again. The thought sent a cold chill into his heart. He recalled previous cases; there had been two killings so far, a third and they had a serial killer on their hands.

And a serial killer would continue until he was stopped.

8

James Drinkwater and Cecil Clay had taken to eating at McDonald's most evenings. For varying reasons. It was scrupulously clean, and both men, in spite of their bachelor scruffiness, were fastidious in that respect. It was in close proximity to both their homes. But above all, the fast food restaurant offered an anonymity that was not to be found in any of the city's cafes. Neither man had any wish to engage in idle conversation with a stranger sharing their table, and they were self-conscious over the possibility of being overheard.

McDonald's was always crowded in the early evening, teenagers snatching a burger before going to the cinema, late leaving office workers revitalizing their flagging brains with a strong coffee. Their company provided a background against which to talk, a younger generation not interested in a couple of middle-aged second-hand booksellers. Nobody here would recognise a Vicar Choral; the majority had little or no interest in cathedral activities.

Mostly for Drinkwater and Clay it was book talk. They discussed prices and marketing; Clay was in the process of preparing a catalogue it would take him several weeks to complete. He was a perfectionist; his honesty demanded a detailed description of the condition of each volume offered for sale. Drinkwater had a catalogue in mind; it was tedious and time consuming. He decided to wait until after the Festival week; if the shop sales had increased then he would have no need to launch into postal selling.

Rarely now did they discuss their schooldays. They had covered most aspects since their re-union; there was little more to add. Any further theories on the deaths of the two organists were to be found in the tabloid newspapers most days.

Frame had been dead for over a fortnight. His funeral service had taken place in the cathedral a couple of days ago.

Michael Corms had played the organ; James Drinkwater had conducted the choir. It was a day that both men would prefer to forget; funerals were depressing at best, and this one had an atmosphere of climbing tension. There were several strangers amongst the congregation; the killer might have been one of them, come to gloat over his mutilation.

Cecil Clay had not attended the service. He still remembered his parents' funerals, and had vowed never to attend another.

Sometimes the two men went their separate ways after their meal; tonight, Drinkwater had specifically asked his friend to return to the shop with him. He had picked up a William Le Queux novel that morning in the charity shop, an 1890 first edition. He would welcome Clay's opinion on pricing. It might be a rarity.

Drinkwater had just inserted the key in the street door when a short, dark-haired man wearing jeans and a sky blue sweatshirt detached himself from a group of window gazers.

"Mr Drinkwater?" The voice was soft yet purposeful, taking care that he was not overheard.

"That's me." Drinkwater turned back, his companion was staring in undisguised curiosity at the stranger. "The shop's closed, but if you'd like to browse, I'll …"

"I'd appreciate a chat with you, if I may, and your friend, too, if he isn't in a hurry. My name's Ford, Detective Sergeant, CID."

"Oh yes …" James Drinkwater was startled. "By all means, do step inside. This is …"

"Mr. Cecil Clay." The name was spoken casually with a nod. "I've seen you about town. I had it in mind to call on you also, but perhaps I can kill two birds with one stone, so to speak."

"Most certainly." Clay was clearly nervous, in danger of tripping over his feet as he stooped inside the shop. There was only one subject that this policeman could possibly want to talk to them about, he had heard that door-to-door enquiries were taking place. The police always made him uneasy, an indoctrination that went back to his schooldays when pupils were punished harshly for minor misdemeanours. Once he had almost walked absent-mindedly out of a bookshop clutching an intended purchase. He might well have been prosecuted for shoplifting; he still had nightmares about it.

"Tea or coffee?" Drinkwater switched on the light in the living accommodation, indicated some straight-backed chairs.

"As it comes, whichever." Ford seated himself, crossed one leg over the other. Such enquiries had to be conducted as informally as possible if they were to bear fruit.

"I was at the funeral," Ford added.

"A sad occasion." The Vicar Choral switched on the kettle, stood by it. "Distressing under normal circumstances, absolutely awful in view of what happened. I hope you catch him soon, Sergeant."

"We'll need help; it won't be easy. I understand Frame was a loner, as was Herbert Poppleton, which reduces the field of acquaintances."

"I never met the man," Clay added quickly, as if to exonerate himself from any possible suspicion. "I don't go to cathedral services."

"It isn't Frame I've come to talk about." Ford accepted a mug of tea. "I need to find out as much as I can about Herbert Poppleton as he was years ago. I understand both of you were in the choir whilst he was organist." A statement, not a question.

"Yes, that's true." Clay swallowed as though he had just made an admission of guilt.

Drinkwater nodded, said, "That's right, I remember him from when I was about fifteen. I never set eyes on him from the day I left, though. He looked old then, he must have been really ancient when he died."

"What was his wife like?" Ford asked.

"I only ever caught odd glimpses of her," Drinkwater answered. "Big, shuffled around, never spoke to anybody. I always remember old Herbert telling us on more than one occasion that in all the time they had been married, he had never seen her in the nude." He laughed, but it sounded forced.

"He wasn't a womaniser, then?"

"Definitely not." Clay slurped his drink. "But, like James, I didn't know Poppleton well. He was an awesome figure. As boys we were terrified of him, small as he was."

"You went to his house?" Ford's gaze alternated between the two of them, finally settled on the Vicar Choral.

"He used to invite us round for tea and scones."

"Individually?"

"Sometimes. But Mrs Poppleton was always in the house, if that's what you're implying."

Cecil Clay licked his lips nervously, stuttered slightly when he spoke. "Er … of course, that's right, she was always around. There was never a … a hint of anything improper."

"I'm sure there wasn't." Ford smiled. "I just needed confirmation. Can either of you think of any reason why anybody should want to kill Herbert Poppleton?"

They couldn't. Nobody could. It was the work of a crazed killer who didn't need a reason. Which was why he might kill again.

* * * * *

Clay had the feeling, that the girl would turn around and face him. She stood there, slightly but sensuously stooped, gazing out of the window. Naked, of course.

Her figure was as near to perfection as any female had the right to expect, her buttocks small and firm, thighs that were symbolic of the maternal instinct. He had never seen her face, but in his mind he pictured it clearly, particularly the eyes. When she turned, as she surely would, her large, mystical eyes would focus unblinkingly on him, follow him wherever he went. Pleading. For what, he did not know.

He was naked, too, standing under the shower with the curtain back so that he could watch her. The feel of the warm water, the way it played upon his bent and sparse frame, excited him.

Ever since he had brought the painting from the exhibition, he had taken to showering three or four times a day, whereas previously this newly discovered erotic pleasure had been nothing more than a necessary chore that he had performed once or twice weekly. His former lingering body odours had never troubled him. Indeed, he had scarcely been aware of them.

He had not intended to hang the picture in the shower room; it had come about by chance. Even wrapped in brown paper, carried beneath his arms, its weight a burden that bowed his spine even more than usual, it had excited him on the journey home. So much so that he knew that the only way to view it fittingly, appraisingly, was unclothed. Yet his conscience troubled him, for to simply have undressed before it would have relegated the matter to sordid voyeurism.

There was a hook on the wall of the bathroom where once a cracked mirror had hung. He looped the cord over it, undressed hurriedly. Then stepped back into the shower cubicle and, leaving the plastic curtain open, he ran the water, adjusted the temperature to suit his mood and body.

Then, as now, the picture glass had begun to mist over with condensation. The girl became an opaque silhouette; the steam gave an illusion of movement. He stared breathlessly; she was starting to turn around. Long fair hair that did not straggle with damp, full lips that smiled seductively. And then she was watching his every movement.

Of course it was *she*, it could be no other, for oft times her wide eyes had watched him from the portrait on that piece of varnished wood that hung from James Drinkwater's living quarters. The very same girl, he knew it would be. An intuition on which he had gambled £75. And his gamble had paid off.

The picture was gone, an opaque square. He sensed her closeness, felt her touch and cried out aloud with pleasure.

Afterwards, towelled and fully clothed, he wiped the glass clear; saw that she was back in that rear view posture. His fingers stroked her tenderly, then he lifted the cord off the hook and carried her gently through to the lounge.

The only other picture in the room had obsessed him in a different way over the years. Revulsion and hatred, but he tolerated it because it was a legacy from his dear parents: a late Victorian oil painting of a gentleman of that era, perhaps it was an ancestor, more likely a picture purchased from a second-hand shop at the time when it was fashionable to hang portraits of staid menfolk on the wall as a reminder of a sexist age. The balding head was far too large and heavy for the wasted shoulders, the expression smug. And Cecil had never liked those eyes, small and sunken; they threatened you with retribution for the sins of the flesh. They trespassed upon your innermost thoughts.

Now those eyes seemed to gaze with lusting hypocrisy upon the back of that beautiful girl, open displeasure because she flaunted her nakedness, burned with a secret inner desire for her body. The man, whoever he was, must go.

With a haste that bordered upon rage, Cecil Clay tore at the frame, snapped the cord, and rushed from the room with it. Outside, in the carport that served as a patio, he fumbled along a concrete ledge until his trembling fingers found that which they were seeking. A kitchen knife, its sharp blade rusted from exposure to the atmosphere.

He grasped the hilt, brandished his dagger in the manner of a footpad threatening a wealthy gentlemen for whom he had lain in wait in a dark alley. Those eyes met his, a momentary pleading, but there would be no mercy.

"And now." Cecil Clay's words were barely comprehensible, he lisped as a string of saliva dangled from his trembling lips. "Shall we sing Psalm 151?"

His fury escalated, reached its peak. A downward slash; the canvas ripped, a jagged hole obliterated the small mouth before it could scream.

Frenziedly, Clay stabbed, gouged out the eyes, sliced away the flared nostrils. Hacking, mouthing obscenities that had never passed his lips before. Destroying something that had dominated his life since boyhood, made him what he was. Finally, when the canvas was gone, he used a foot to snap the wooden frame, stood bowed and trembling over the scattered remains.

Always fastidiously tidy, he stooped and gathered up the broken wood and the frayed material, deposited them in the dustbin and replaced the lid firmly; checked it in case a gust of wind should dislodge it and allow that monstrosity to escape.

Back indoors, he washed his hands in the sink, went through to the lounge. The girl stood with her back towards him but he sensed the relief that emanated from her bare body. As though she was relaxed now that that lusting old man had been removed from close proximity.

Cecil Clay smiled to himself. Now he had this beautiful unknown girl all to himself. Later on, when his body had revitalised itself, he would carry her back upstairs. And he would shower again.

He remembered again the painting of her face, which hung in his friend's home. On more than one occasion he had hinted to Drinkwater of a possible purchase, or even an exchange deal for some saleable books. But always the other had shaken his head, embarrassed by his refusal to part with the girl.

But now Cecil no longer needed that similar picture, for when the glass on his own misted with condensation, and his frail body trembled with passion, she turned to face him. And came to him.

He shook with excitement because he had also exacted an overdue revenge upon one who had dominated him for so many years.

9

"Michael, I've *got* to have some money!" There was desperation in Sandra's voice as she came through from the kitchen, saw that her husband was already changed in preparation for his nightly session at the pub.

"I gave you twenty yesterday!" Indignation, there was no hint of guilt.

"And you borrowed fifteen back to go to the pub!" She screwed the tea towel up into a ball.

"What've you spent the five pounds on?" His expression was aggressive, accusing.

"Food, for starters," she snapped. "The chicken we had for tea tonight cost four quid, not to mention the veg and the pudding. And little Michael needs a new pair of shoes, just in case you hadn't noticed that the soles are coming adrift."

"Put it in the book, then." His sarcasm camouflaged any hint of guilt that he might have felt. "Since you went on that book-keeping course, I hope your arithmetic has improved!"

"See for yourself, then." She reached a small cashbook from by the telephone, opened it up, and held it out for him to see. "Including the fifteen you took back last night, and not counting the remaining sixty pounds you owe on this week's housekeeping," she tapped the relevant page, "currently, Michael, you are in debt to me for the sum of one hundred and eighty seven pounds!"

"Well, that certainly proves something." He smirked.

"What?"

"You've managed admirably, so I must've been paying you too much in the past."

She fought back a retort, her eyes watered. Rarely had she stood up to her husband in the past. A thought crossed her mind: Gerald, so strong and confident, so kind. She would not have to put up with this forever. Suddenly four years seemed an eternity, and she knew she could not hold out that long. Little Michael would be all right—he had to be. "I see," she said, "so I'm not going to be paid the arrears?"

"An assistant organist doesn't earn a lot." He had never confided his salary in her.

"Enough to keep him in drink every night of the week, though."

"I don't drink a lot. One pint, two at the most."

"Another thing." She felt her confidence surge, sensed that he was backing down.

"Yes?"

"You're in this house for about an hour every day. You come back from the cathedral, go up to your study, and work until the meal's ready. Then, as soon as you've eaten, you're off to the pub. The kids have noticed it. In fact, Julie commented on it."

"I've just been up and said goodnight to them."

"And what's happening about my car?" She sensed an advantage; pushed for everything she could think of.

"The assessor's going to look at it on Tuesday. Then we'll know whether the insurance will write it off or pay for it to be repaired."

"And if they write it off?"

"I'll buy it back off them and Wally will do a good knock-out job, you'll never even know it's had a bump."

"And you'll settle with me out of the write-off cheque, won't you, Michael?"

"I'll work something out." He edged towards the door.

"When?"

"I'll see how things go." He paused, rested his hands on the doorknob. "Oh, and I've got an axe to grind, too, San."

"Have you?" She took a deep breath, held it. Michael always retaliated; you never got away with anything with him. "What's that?"

"Sex." He eyed her steadily; the smirk was back on his face. "I begin to wonder if it will ever happen again."

"If you stayed home on the odd evening, or even came back at a respectable hour, it might." She hoped he wouldn't take her up on that; she would feel guilty. It would be a betrayal of Gerry, the way things were now.

"You're always asleep. Or too tired. Or something."

"I don't like being woken up for sex."

"I think you're getting it somewhere else." His eyes fixed unwaveringly on her.

"How dare you!" Sandra's heart seemed to flip, her legs felt rubbery. She sensed cold perspiration on her forehead.

"It's just a thought," he laughed.

"A diversion, so that we don't have to discuss unpleasant subjects. Like money."

"I told you, assistants don't earn a lot."

"Well, you're acting organist until after the Festival so things have to look up temporarily."

"I don't get paid any extra for doing Frame's job. It's considered an honour."

She was watching him carefully, now she sensed something in him that she had never seen before: an uneasiness, a nervousness. Lying didn't affect him that way; there was definitely something disturbing him. She said, "They might just appoint you organist full-time."

"I don't think so." It came out in a rush.

"You don't want the job?"

He licked his lips, averted his gaze. "After what's happened to Rupert? And Poppleton? I'd have to be crazy."

"Somebody will continue to play the organ in the cathedral, they won't suspend services. I thought you always wanted to be an organist, Michael? I didn't think you were the type to get cold feet."

"I'm not, I'm just thinking of you. And the kids. I won't be any good to anybody if I go and get topped."

She sighed. He had turned everything to his advantage, as usual. He was scared, all right, but it was a good excuse for not taking on a demanding job. All Michael wanted was enough money to enable him to go to the pub every night, and if he could get away with paying her as little as possible, have his children looked after and his food on the table, that was fine by him. Well, he was in for a shock soon. She must talk to Gerry, tell him she was ready whenever he wanted her.

"I'd better be going." Corms edged the front door open, stood there hesitantly. "I wish I knew who was doing it, San."

"So does everybody else. I guess, *if* they catch him, it'll turn out to be some psycho with a record, probably set free on parole by some crazy judge. Somebody we've never heard of."

"It has to be somebody we know." His features were pale; the fingers on the doorknob shook slightly. "Somebody who, for some crazy reason, has it in for organists. Lichfield Cathedral organists."

"Maybe, but in Poppleton's case they left it an awful long time. He'd been gone from here five years."

"Maybe we'll move on after the Festival" He stepped out into the street, "I've heard there's a couple of posts going. Or I might even go back to teaching."

Sandra stood there, experienced a sense of triumph. She hadn't got any money out of him, that was too much to hope for, but by the time the Festival was over, she would be gone from here.

Later she would phone Gerry.

10

Canon Feiffer was angry. He had been angry for the past couple of days for a variety of reasons.

Charlesworth, the headmaster, was attempting to fob him off over the incident of those dreadful boys focusing binoculars on Mrs Feiffer's bedroom window. The culprits had claimed upon being questioned that a nest of starlings had hatched out in the eaves and they had been studying the fledglings with their lenses. Poppycock! Worse, the headmaster believed them, he had even been along to check for himself, and there were some baby birds up there. He had apologised for the nuisance and stressed that he had instructed the boys not to focus their binoculars on the precentor's house again.

Feiffer tore the letter into shreds, showered it in the direction of the waste paper basket. The boys were liars; they were cunning enough to find a plausible excuse for their disgusting voyeurism. Worse, Charlesworth actually believed them. Neither the bishop's nor the dean's secretary had had the courtesy to reply to the precentor's letter.

And that policeman had called this morning. Without a prior appointment, what a dashed cheek! The fellow wasn't even dressed befitting the force, a sweatshirt and a pair of grubby jeans. Ford, his name was; Feiffer scribbled it on his jotter. He might write a letter to the chief constable and point out how sloppy the police were becoming.

The detective had implied by innuendo that Feiffer might have known the killer, that it might be somebody connected with the cathedral. And those questions Ford had asked about Herbert Poppleton were preposterous. Slanderous, in fact. Could Herbert have had homosexual tendencies? Not Herbert—a man of his standing would not have stooped to such depths. It was unthinkable. And he most certainly would not have been a womaniser. Had he not told everybody on numerous occasions that in fifty years of marriage he had never seen his wife naked? So why should he want to view any other woman unclothed?

Jobs for the boys, that was the trouble with the police. That fellow Ford should be out there hunting the murderer, not making insulting suggestions about Herbert's morality. Feiffer had told the detective as much, in no uncertain terms.

Something else angered Feiffer, but it had not occurred to him until now. The night on which Rupert Frame had been murdered, Lumby had deserted his post, gone to fetch fish and chips from the shop downtown. Had the Verger remained in the cathedral then in all probability the organist would still be alive today. Lumby had been disciplined, a written warning, no more. Was night duty being observed or was it being shirked? That was Homer's responsibility; he was Head Verger.

Feiffer decided to make an unscheduled visit to the cathedral in order to find out if the late duties were being observed. If there was nobody around and the north transept was unlocked, then he would ensure that Homer was sacked. The fellow was not suitable for the job. Feiffer had disliked him over the years; this was his chance to rid the cathedral of him once and for all.

The precentor waited until dusk. He had no fears of the dark, and anyway, the murderer was only interested in organists, all the newspapers confirmed that. Just a quick check. If a verger was on duty, fair enough, if not …

He left the house with his well-known shambling gait, arms swinging by his sides, cheeks inflating and deflating. It was a balmy evening, sweat trickled down his wide forehead, stinging his eyes. He paused, fumbled a handkerchief from his pocket, mopped his brow and wiped his spectacles. Voices, laughter had him peering into the gathering dusk.

Dashed if there weren't still tourists in the Close! A group were clustered by the well, one of them pointing towards the cathedral. "That's where the murder was done. It's locked up now, but we'll be able to go take a look tomorrow."

Anger shook the precentor again. That was all these people had come for, to gawp and drool over a scene of bloody murder. *The Mercury* had claimed an influx of tourists due to the killing; one of the tabloids—so Feiffer had heard, he wouldn't read such trash—had headlined it, "Thomas Becket in Lichfield Cathedral." The tourist board would not admit it, but Feiffer knew it all right, saw it as a boost for tourism. It was an ill wind …

With some difficulty he negotiated the wide flight of steps down to the north door. He tried the handle, the door swung inwards. Whoever was on duty should have kept it locked; those ghouls out there might well trespass in search of the murder scene. It was the duty Verger's job to lock the door behind him once he was inside; clearly this task had been overlooked lately.

Feiffer listened but there were no strains of organ music coming from within. Because Rupert Frame was dead and his temporary replacement preferred the evils of alcohol to the holiness of the house of God.

Corms would have to go after the Festival, Feiffer was determined upon that. There was a meeting scheduled for early August to discuss the appointment of a new organist. The precentor intended to put his own case strongly; a new assistant must be appointed also. Corms must be dismissed. Not only did the man lack dedication, never mind obvious talents, but he was a drunkard who brought the Church into disrepute. Also there were rumours about his wife; Feiffer would not mention those unless more substantial evidence came to light in the meantime.

The dim lighting cast weird shadows, patches of blackness that might have hidden a lurking killer. His own footsteps sounded hollow, echoed eerily as he walked across the nave, paused to bow to the altar.

May God have mercy upon my soul. And Rupert's and Herbert's, too. He felt his heartbeat, a sudden twinge made him wince. He hesitated. This was foolishness; the cathedral was deserted, whichever verger was on duty had left his post, left the place unlocked. They must be punished for their negligence.

Feiffer walked down towards the south transept door. Perhaps that was unlocked, too. He clicked the handle, but the heavy door would not budge. Anyway, a cathedral's weakness was one unlocked door no matter how secure the rest.

His misted vision alighted on a square of Stygian blackness that nestled in the wall. It might have been the entrance to a bottomless pit; it seemed so sinister in the deep gloom. Or a dungeon where Cromwell had cast his prisoners during the siege, their skeletons still lying twisted on the floor. Or a secret passageway like the one that had once run from the bishop's palace.

No, it was none of these; his imagination was running riot. Behind that low oaken door lay a flight of steps that went upwards, a spiral staircase that twisted its way skywards inside the great central spire. From aloft, through the arched windows, an unparalleled view of the city and its surrounding landscape was afforded the privileged sightseer. Nowadays, only the fortunate few were permitted to embark upon this tour of breathtaking scenery. Vertigo was the price asked; all but steeplejacks and mountaineers clung dizzily to the handrail at a height of 258 feet above ground.

Feiffer had scaled it once in his early days here; even as a young man he had refused a second invitation. The memory of that trip had his equilibrium threatening to orbit. The authorities were wise to keep that door locked; the central spire was an ideal setting for a spectacular suicide.

He walked back, bowed again to the altar before turning his back upon it and shuffling westwards down the nave. Above him, stained glass windows cast kaleidoscopic patterns on the architecture as they reflected the last light of a saffron sky and the dazzling exterior illuminations of the Close.

He was curious to know whom the duty Verger was. The roster book, kept on a shelf by the Head Verger's desk just inside the west doors, would tell him. He needed the exact information in order to press for the sacking of the culprit. Having ascertained that fact, he promised himself that he would leave. And he would write the necessary letter before retiring for the night. The desk area was in deep shadow, a kind of partition behind rows of stacked hymn and prayer books. He wished that he had brought a torch; the subdued lighting did not infiltrate here. But he knew where the book was kept, he could find it by feel, take it into a patch of light to scan the pages until …

"Good evening, Precentor."

Feiffer started, almost cried out. The pain in his chest stabbed him briefly, left him breathless. A figure, a Stygian silhouette, rose up behind the desk, a nemesis whose features were corpse-like in the darkness. A smile that was sensed rather than seen, skeletal fingers gripping the desktop.

"*Homer*!" Feiffer wheezed.

"Yes, sir?"

"What are you doing here?"

"I've taken over from the duty Verger, sir. Needes went home sick only a few minutes ago. Why, is there anything wrong?"

"No …no … Yes, there is, Homer. The north transept door is unlocked."

"Yes, Precentor, Needes left that way, I have his key. I was just on my way to lock it."

"Oh, I see." Disappointment because there were no grounds for a written complaint.

"It's unusual to find you in here at such an hour, sir."

"I … I just wanted to look around. After the tourists had left. I thought there would be more light than this in here."

"I can switch the lights on for you, sir, if you wish."

"No, no, Homer, it doesn't matter." *Because I don't feel well enough to stay any longer.*

"They've removed the tent now, sir." The Head Verger's eyes seemed to glow in the darkness.

"The tent? Oh, you mean the tarpaulins they erected in the south transept for restoration work?"

"No, Precentor, I am referring to the one in the organ loft. The one erected by the police in their search for clues. The cleaners did a magnificent job, removed most of the traces of blood, but there are still a few stains visible if you look hard enough. Would you care to take a look, Precentor?"

"*No!*" The word came out as a throaty scream.

"Pilgrims came to view the bloodstains of Thomas Becket in Canterbury Cathedral, sir. A kind of memorial to a holy man, don't you think? Rupert Frame may never have a monument erected to him, sir, but there will always be traces of his blood remaining where it has seeped between the stonework. Do let me give you a glimpse, Precentor."

"No. You're mad, Homer."

"Perhaps, sir, but we're all mad in our different ways, aren't we? Take this murderer, he's mad. Evil. He has to be, doesn't he, to do what he did to Rupert Frame? And to Herbert Poppleton. And he enjoyed every second of it; it was doubtless the biggest thrill of his life. A sexual crime, the ultimate in perversion. I can understand him, sir, even if I can't condone his crime."

Feiffer backed away a couple of paces, lost his balance and almost fell. "I … don't … want … to … see, Homer."

"Very well, Precentor, but I think you should see where a devoted servant of the cathedral died. He shed his blood in the services of God, no man can give a greater sacrifice than to …"

"Stop it, Homer!"

"I'm sorry, sir."

"I'm going now, Homer." Still backing away, afraid to turn his back upon the other. The sharp pain in his chest had intensified; his vision had blurred so that the Verger's silhouette was quivering like a reflection in a pool of water.

"As you wish, sir. Would you like me to escort you to the door?"

"No."

"I have to lock it after you, sir."

Feiffer bumped against a pew, managed to regain his balance.

"You can sense murder in the atmosphere, can't you, sir?" Homer's nostrils flared, he sniffed the air. "A kind of cloying smell. Like blood, in fact. I guess it will always remain; the vibes of violent death are strong. You can almost believe that the murderer is still in here, hiding somewhere. You ask yourself where, glance all around you, peer fearfully into the shadows. A trick of the light, an unrecognisable noise has your heart pounding, your pulse racing. You think you see him crouching in the darkness, you can't be sure. You fight against the urge to run. Nowhere is safe."

"Stop it!" the Precentor screamed. It echoed up to the roof, hung there. He thought he heard Homer laugh. Feiffer turned, he had to force every muscle in his body to function. It was as though leaden balls were chained to his ankles. His breath came in stentorian gasps. He could barely see now, his vision was streaked with scarlet.

Don't follow me, Homer!

Homer was following him, slow footsteps that kept pace with his own staggerings, but he dared not glance back. Only an instinctive sense of direction kept him on course—he had trodden these flagstones for forty years. He turned left at the end of the nave, headed into the north transept.

"Are you sure you wouldn't care for a quick look in the organ loft, Precentor?"

Feiffer fought against the pain, blind fear kept him going. He wanted to yell back, 'It's you, isn't it, Homer? *You* killed him, you killed them both. Didn't you?' But he had no breath for verbal accusations.

Somehow he made it to the door, fell against it as he pushed it open. Outside, the illuminations dazzled him. He wondered if he had the strength to mount the steps.

The youths who had been over by the well had moved and now stood in a group by the old deanery entrance. One said, "Hey, look, there's an old guy just come out of the cathedral. Looks like 'e's been drinking."

Raucous laughter.

Canon Feiffer stumbled and fell. He banged his head on one of the steps, grunted and tasted blood. It smelled just like Homer had said.

"There 'e goes, down for the count."

More raucous laughter.

"We can't *leave* 'im there," somebody protested. "Pick 'im up and sit 'im up agin the wall over there."

They walked down the steps to where the sprawled form lay, hands reached out for the limp arms and legs.

"Christ, 'e's a bloody weight!"

"Lift 'im up, then."

Somehow they struggled back up the steps, panted and grunted their way over to the brick deanery wall. It was only when they attempted to sit the unconscious man up against the brickwork and his head slumped forward that realization slowly dawned upon them.

One of them said, "Jesus, e's bloody dead!"

11

"If it's any consolation to you," Ford said, "Feiffer died from natural causes. A heart attack. He'd had heart trouble for some years, apparently."

"It is." There was no mistaking the fleeting expression of relief on Michael Corms's face.

Ford refrained from adding that the precentor's dead features had been frozen in an expression of sheer terror. That was better kept quiet for the moment for a lot of reasons; it might not even have any bearing on police investigations. There were no logical grounds for suspicion; Borman had emphasised that to the press.

Just Ford's gut feeling and he was keeping a tight rein on that for the moment. This was no time for playing wild hunches. Charles Homer had stated that Feiffer seemed to be in good health and spirits when he had left the cathedral that night. But why had the canon gone on a tour of inspection at that hour?

"I've already been interviewed about Rupert Frame's death." Corms's protruding ears turned a shade of pink. Next thing, they would be accusing *him*.

"This isn't exactly an interrogation." Ford knew how to smile reassuringly; there were times when you got what you wanted out of people by appearing casual. This was one of those times. "I'm attempting to build up a profile."

"Of the killer?"

"Yes, but also of organists in general. I need to find out what makes them tick, and, hopefully, what might make somebody want to kill and mutilate them. I haven't ruled out a sexual motive."

"The guy's probably just a psycho. Look at some of the famous cases that have made the headlines: Dahmer, Nilsen, the Russian cannibal, the Black Mantis, that guy they called 'The Hangman.' "

"You've read up on them." Not a flicker of his shrewd

eyes betrayed Ford's surprise.

"Morbid interest, I guess." Corms was suddenly uneasy. "I used to read horror novels, but nowadays I just read the newspapers. I don't see how I can help you, Sergeant, this guy doesn't have to have a reason, does he?"

"Not a reason, a *cause*, something that triggers off the urge inside him to kill, maybe something that happened as far back as his childhood. Find that and we're halfway to finding the killer."

"I don't see how I can help you."

"Neither do I right now, but it may be that you can tell me something which might seem meaningless to you but it's what I'm looking for. Tell me a bit about yourself."

"Me? Oh, all right, not that I've had a very interesting life. I took a Latin and music degree at Birmingham University. After I graduated, I went on to teach music at Wrekin. Teaching wasn't my vocation, though, but I stuck with it for ten years, then I saw the assistant organist's job was vacant here. I applied and got it. Rupert Frame had been here about two and a half years, then. I guess that's all there is to tell, really."

"How did you get on with Rupert Frame?"

"Detective Sergeant Clifford quizzed me on that." Corms was suspicious again.

"I'm just interested to know. Like I said, I need to know a lot about organists."

"I got on okay with him. That about sums it up. I neither liked nor disliked him, and I think he felt the same about me. We had a working relationship; we never met socially. The only time I've ever been inside his house was on the day of the interview. If I needed to ask him anything outside working hours, I either phoned him or went round to his place. I never got beyond the front porch. Rupert was dedicated to his job, he never once put upon me. If anything, it was just the reverse."

"Can you think of any enemies he might have had?"

"No, he wasn't the kind to make enemies. If you disliked

him, you did so at a distance. He just got on with his job. He wasn't a conversationalist. If you met him out and about, he just passed the time of day. If he had anything to tell you, he told you. He was abrupt but you knew it was just his way, nothing personal. I doubt if anybody outside his family has ever got close to him. His biggest disappointment was his son. The boy was regularly in trouble with the police, still is. If you ask me, Adrian's a corner flag short of a football pitch. Whatever his father was, his son is the exact opposite. Have you met him, Sergeant?"

"I've still that pleasure to come." Jason Ford was thoughtful. "Do you know how father and son got on?"

"Only what I've heard, and as I've said, Rupert wasn't one to disclose anything of a personal nature. They say that Rupert did everything humanly possible to help the boy. He took him to several psychiatrists, once to a hypnotherapist. The boy resented it; after each attempt to help him, he retaliated immediately. A fight, shoplifting—anything that would drag his father's name through the mud. He seemed hell-bent on tarnishing the family's reputation. Everything was, and still is, due to drugs, I reckon. He's been busted for them more than once. Drugs can make you do things out of character, can't they, Sergeant? They cause a personality change. Take that woman shopper who was stabbed in a busy shopping precinct the other week. She didn't even know her attacker; he just got an urge to stick a knife in her. The papers said the killer was high on crack. Now, just suppose this bloke who is killing organists has a crack addiction, it would account for the murders and mutilations, wouldn't it, Sergeant?"

"It might," Ford agreed. It was at the top of his list of possibilities, had been right from the start. But he had a hunch that there was more to this than drugs alone. "But you've helped me to form a general profile of an organist, Mr Corms, and that could be very helpful in the future. Tell me, how does James Drinkwater fit into the cathedral scene?"

"He doesn't, frankly." Corms smiled guiltily, he was not in the habit of gossiping about other members of the cathedral. "He's a misfit. Like Frame in a way. Odd bloke, got a good voice, knows his job. Feiffer didn't like him, though. I think the feeling was mutual, so Homer told me. Not that one can believe everything that Homer says."

"Oh?"

"Oh, just petty suspicions, not even rumours. Some of the choir had been visiting Drinkwater at his place; I guess it happens at most cathedrals. Maybe I should have some of them back to my place, but when you've got four kids of your own, you never get round to it. Anyway, Feiffer got to know and carpeted Drinkwater. At least, he spoke to him about it. The precentor was one to bear a grudge; in his eyes, the Vicar Choral was up to something sordid and that was that. Feiffer didn't like Homer, either; they'd had a sort of feud for years. You know, ignoring each other, Feiffer was looking for every fault he could find with Homer and so on. But as for Drinkwater, I've always found him pleasant enough. I think he's lazy, but he does his job in the cathedral so that's none of my business."

"And Clay?"

"Well, what can I say?" Corms laughed aloud. "The general opinion of him is that he smells, he pinches girls' bottoms, and he's a general bloody nuisance to the community."

"Has he a record of sexual assaults?"

"Oh, no, maybe I shouldn't have put it like that. He once—perhaps accidentally—touched a girl's bottom in a shop and she slapped his face. Nobody's ever forgotten it; it's a standing joke. But he did recently cause a titter by paying seventy-five quid for a nude painting from an art exhibition. If he'd just walked in and bought it, nobody would have batted an eye. But he tried to create an obvious smoke cover, rang up and asked for it to be wrapped up, walked around the gallery until it was empty before picking it up. This city thrives on petty gossip, you know. But I'll vouch that he does smell. BO, and very strong. Take a tip from me, Sergeant, don't stand too close to him! And if you get talking to him in the street, it's like trying to shake the old man of the sea off your back. A lot of folks cross over the road when they spot him coming. But Drinkwater doesn't seem to mind, they were old school friends and they both sell books. So they've obviously got plenty in common. I guess people talk about them, but myself, I couldn't be bothered. I mean, a guy who gets his thrills out of paintings of nude women isn't likely to be gay, is he? Not that it's any reflection of him if he is; I'm just making a point. I think both Drinkwater and Clay are very lonely and that's the basis of their friendship. If they'd got the courage they'd probably join a lonely hearts club, except that they're too set in their bachelor ways. Oddities but quite harmless, that's how I see them."

"Thank you, Mr Corms." Ford stood up, "I'm most grateful for what you've told me. You never know, somewhere amongst it all, you might have given me some valuable information." He moved closer to the door.

"Sergeant?" Michael Corms was suddenly nervous again, glancing towards the stairway in case any of the children might be out of bed and listening. Sandra had gone down to the shop for a jar of coffee; as soon as she returned, he would get out. Tonight he was due at the Shoulder of Mutton; he always went there on Thursdays.

"Yes?"

"I'm taking over as organist until a full time replacement is appointed …"

"I see." *And you're shit scared right now. Jesus Christ, how do you tell a guy he's not likely to get topped when he's stepped right into the firing line?*

"I shall have to do some evening practices next week—the Festival's only ten days away. Everything has to go to perfection."

Ford smiled reassuringly; it was a con, made him feel guilty. Because he knew the risks as well as Corms did.

Better, in fact.

"There will be a police presence." It sounded vague, a kind of half promise. "Just as there was at Frame's funeral. Every cathedral service has a plain clothes officer in the congregation, and there are round-the-clock vigils in the Close. I don't think the killer will strike again in Lichfield." He had to boost the organist's confidence—that was the least he could do. There were several thousand tourists in the area for the Festival and more were arriving daily; the murderer had the cover he needed. The police could only do their best. Somebody had to play the organ in the cathedral. It happened to be Corms; he would be protected as far as was possible. Policemen were only human. But Ford could not tell the other that.

"Thank you, Sergeant." Michael Corms seemed relieved.

"I'll see you around. I may need to talk to you again," Ford said, and stepped back outside into the evening sunshine. It was as if the balmy atmosphere had lost some of its warmth. It could just have been that summer was well advanced, that the nights were turning cooler. But Ford knew a hunch when he felt one. The killer had not left; he was still around, still in the city.

Waiting.

And Corms was Ford's bait.

12

Ford had never liked paperwork, but he had accepted it as an integral part of the job, a compilation of facts that often knitted together and threw up a vital piece of information which otherwise might have gone unnoticed.

He was meticulous in this respect. Most evenings he stored fresh facts on his laptop, used his own private filing systems in conjunction with police computer files. The organist killings were going to use up several discs.

"Anything new?" Brenda leaned across him, set a mug of tea down on the desk.

"We'll see in a minute." He was tired; the late July heat had taken its toll on him today. The computer whirred, asked the user to wait one minute.

"Clay?" She kissed her husband on the cheek.

"No, I haven't got a lot on him so far. All hearsay: voyeurism, possibly bisexual. The computer can't make up its mind, it needs more facts. Same goes for Drinkwater."

"Who, then?"

"Homer, Charles." It was as if the software heard her, answered her question spontaneously.

Age: 77

Occupation: Head Verger, Lichfield Cathedral

Duration of Employment: 1961–64, 1966–

Description: Greying hair, Balding, Height 5.10, Powerful, reputed to hold black belt

Convictions: None

Suspicions: Believed to have been involved with S&M group in Essex c1964

Territorial Army service: 1964–1966

Marital status: Divorced

Enemies: Canon George Feiffer, Precentor (deceased)

Rupert J. Frame, Organist (deceased)
Petty feuds

"There you go, then." Brenda read the file through. "A nasty man, a pervert, and his enemies have both recently died."

"One from natural causes."

"The other was murdered and sexually mutilated. Homer was suspected of being into kinky sex. He disliked Frame. Seems to me he's your number one suspect."

"My hunch says 'no.' "

"Your hunch could be wrong. What was his quarrel with Frame?"

"A general resentment of authority. Two of the other vergers, Needes and Lumby, confirmed that independently. Homer has also, apparently, transferred his dislike to Corms. It will doubtless be passed on to the new organist when he's appointed. Homer's like that. I haven't discarded him." Ford sipped his tea, looked thoughtful, "My main worry is why the north transept door was left unlocked on the evenings of both deaths."

"Lumby had gone for fish and chips when Frame was murdered, you know that."

"Yes, sheer carelessness. But on the night Feiffer had a heart attack outside, Homer was inside, although he had not locked the door behind him as is the inflexible rule, and he's a stickler for the rule book."

"Maybe he just forgot."

"Or else he was expecting somebody."

"Feiffer?"

"Unlikely. I'm told that the precentor almost never went into the cathedral in the evenings except when there was a rehearsal. There wasn't one on that night—it had taken place earlier, immediately after evensong."

"Who, then?"

"Darling." Ford switched off the screen, twisted round to meet her lips. "That is what I have to find out. And I'm damned sure Charles Homer isn't going to tell me.

Incidentally, it was Hebert Poppleton who recommended Homer for the job. And it was Poppleton who persuaded him to come back to the cathedral after his TA service. And they both came from Essex originally."

"Could be they were both into S&M, then?"

"That's guesswork, but it's a possibility. Two perverts who quarrelled. But Frame most certainly wasn't into kinky sex, so we're back to the original organist link. And now Corms is in the hot seat and scared shitless."

"It's only three days to the Festival."

"Precisely, and that makes me think we're running out of time. If the murderer thrives on notoriety, then what better time to make his third strike? And when that happens, we are up against a serial killer."

Jason Ford stood up, pulled a dust cover over his computer. "I'm going out," he said, refraining from adding, 'I might be some time.' That quip had worn thin during his three years of marriage.

Brenda did not ask where or when she might expect him back. Her own period of service in the force had taught her that CID officers did not work to a time schedule.

However, she was not immune from concern. Only too well she recalled the Black Mantis and the one they had dubbed "The Hangman." One more killing and it might not be deemed lucky for Ford.

* * * * *

"I think we might vary the eating establishment occasionally, don't you?" Cecil Clay picked at his French fries, grimaced through a mouthful of burger. "I mean, it gets much of a muchness, doesn't it?"

"The Kabin closes at five." James Drinkwater stared at his Filet-O-Fish. "There's nowhere much after then, even during the Festival. Hotels come expensive. We could try takeaways."

"The pleasure of eating out is eating *out*." The other

ruffled his hair with greasy fingers, surreptitiously wiped them on his trousers, glanced almost guiltily in the direction of the tissues in the wall box.

"Remember that bloody awful school food?"

"I certainly do." Clay's expression was thoughtful. "Teatime, in particular. Two slices of thick bread, butter scratched on and off, you had to provide your own jam. My favourite was chocolate spread—Mother used to get it from the corner shop. Tea out of the big urn. Funny thing," he sipped from his polystyrene cup, smacked his lips noisily, "this tastes much the same, I never noticed it before."

"It comes out of an urn."

"Yes, yes, that must be why." Cecil was thoughtful for a moment; his eyes seemed to film over. "That painting of yours, James …"

"Which isn't for sale or exchange."

"No, no, of course not, I would not presume to ask again. But … does it turn you on?"

Drinkwater winced; the other's whisper was like a shout. Some youths sitting at the next table jerked their heads round, stared rudely, thought they must have misheard. "It's very artistic."

"I brought a similar one quite recently." Clay leaned across the table "I'd swear it was the same girl. She's standing with her back towards you."

"How do you know it's the same one?" Drinkwater fidgeted with embarrassment. The youths were still staring.

"I *know* it is."

"All right, I'll take your word for it."

"Suppose we go back to my place so you can see for yourself?"

"I've got some postal orders to pack up."

"I'd like you to come." It was almost a plea.

"Oh, all right, then, but I mustn't stop long."

Clay's home was less than ten minutes' walk from Dam Street, a neat bungalow almost hidden behind an untrimmed privet hedge. Cecil was no gardener, and the straggling lawn confirmed that. Indoors there was a meticulous tidiness that bordered on the obsessional, in total contrast to his personal appearance.

He shrugged himself out of the frayed mac, brushed it with his hand before hanging it on a peg. The carpets were old and worn, vacuumed frequently, and ornaments were placed symmetrically rather than artistically. Books were stacked on the floor in even piles like a young child might build with toy bricks.

"Well, what do you think of it?" Clay stabbed a finger in the direction of the fireplace, head thrust forward in the manner of some hunting beast which had just scented its prey.

James Drinkwater stared at the picture. The girl had a kind of arrogance about her, he decided, the way she turned her back and didn't care whether or not you looked. If she turned you on, that was your fault; she wasn't interested. She had probably posed with that attitude, bored, only concerned with the hourly rate.

"It's the same girl, isn't it, James?" Affirmative seeking, *please say* that it is.

"It could well be." Not a chance, but if the other chose to think that then it would be cruel to disillusion him.

"Of course it is. I'm certain of it."

Cecil had to be bloody mad to pay seventy-five quid for that! The artist would probably have come down to fifty in a haggle; even then it was overpriced for what it was. Still, everybody to their taste. Drinkwater's gaze roved the room; it was all a question of what turned you on.

"I'd've given you a hundred for that one of yours," Clay was still staring fixedly at the girl, willing her to turn around. "Still, I won't be so rude as to ask you again, James. I couldn't afford it now, anyway." He turned away, lifted a pile of books off an armchair. "Do sit down."

"I can't stay long." Drinkwater lowered himself into the chair, felt the springs sag.

"Do you remember PJ?" A sudden question, as if he had

to forcibly divorce his attention from the painting and needed a diversion.

"Who could forget him? He was almost as big a bully as Wilson himself. He taught me maths, which is why I failed my O level. You were in that class, weren't you, Cecil?"

"Indeed, I was." A sudden nostalgic anger had Clay's features suffusing with blood, his eyes blazed. "Do you recall that occasion, James?" His fists clenched, the knuckles whitened. "When he threw that board duster at Tolsen? It missed, hit me in the eye, I had a shiner for a week afterwards. And all he said was, 'Well, that'll ensure that you don't doze off for the rest of the lesson, Clay.' And he went on to become Headmaster after Wilson retired!"

"He's probably dead now."

"No, he isn't, I looked him up in Crockford's."

James sighed, it seemed that his companion looked everybody up in Crockford's directory.

"He's retired, still takes services in the village where he lives when the curate's on holiday."

"I see."

"I destroyed the other painting, you know."

"Which painting?"

"The one that hung *there*!" The finger stabbed again, impatient because its visitor did not remember. "You must have noticed it."

"Oh yes, I think I did."

"Dreadful, it was; I can't imagine what possessed my parents to buy it. Perhaps it was given to them by relatives or friends and they hung it up because they were afraid of causing offence."

"Possibly."

"Didn't you think the likeness was uncanny? It could even have been a portrait of himself."

"Who? PJ?"

"No, no, *no*!" Clay banged a fist into his hand. "Nothing like PJ. It was a spit of old Poppleton."

"Oh yes, now you mention it, there was a likeness."

Drinkwater had never really looked at the picture in question.

"It gave me the creeps, it was like he was hanging up there watching your every move. For my parents' sake, I kept it. But it was after I brought the girl that I knew I couldn't keep it any longer. It was as though … as though old Herbert Poppleton disapproved of her nakedness." He gave a short, almost hysterical laugh. "I didn't just throw it out, James, I slashed it to ribbons with a knife then stuffed it in the dustbin. It's gone now, thank God—the dustbin men took it away on Thursday, ground it to a pulp in their cart!"

"Herbert wasn't a bad old stick, just obsessed with his music and the composers."

"He was vile; if he'd been on the teaching staff he would have been worse than Wilson and PJ rolled together."

"I got on all right with him."

"Did he ever get you to sing … Psalm 151?" The question was direct as if the answer was something for which Clay had been seeking over the last thirty-eight years.

"What? There isn't such a psalm. There are only a hundred and fifty psalms." The other was momentarily taken aback.

Clay laughed, it became a childish giggle. "Oh, never mind, James. Just a joke. A silly joke. One of old Herbert's, but if you never heard it, it doesn't matter. Now, let me make you a cup of tea before you go, if you really are in a rush …"

"I really must be going." Drinkwater stood up, fidgeted nervously, "I have to get those orders put up tonight. But feel free to call round tomorrow evening."

"I will," Clay enthused, "Surely, I will. So long as we don't have to sing Psalm 151." He laughed, but this time it sounded forced.

13

The chief took the Festival security briefing himself, a gathering of both uniformed and CID officers in the conference room at the rear of the Rykneld Street HQ. That in itself was indicative to Ford how seriously the force was taking the killings. Last year Borman had conducted the proceedings; it had just been routine.

Detective Chief Superintendent John Anson was a stocky, humourless figure up on the platform, the eyes behind those rimless glasses roamed the room as he spoke, missing nobody. If you thought you could hide in the crowd, you were mistaken.

"We must give priority to musical performances." Anson glanced briefly at the program in his hand. "Beginning with the blues band in the Arts Centre. Every officer will be detailed specifically, we cannot overlook anything. In particular we must concentrate on those events scheduled to take place in the cathedral itself. We must not presume anything, nothing must be taken for granted; the Festival will be prime time for the killer to strike. A murderer of this nature has an ego; he will go for maximum publicity, press reports to gloat over. We don't know his motive—in all probability he has none—and that makes it all the more difficult for us. All I can say is maximum vigilance at all times whilst keeping a low profile."

For a few seconds the chief's eyes met Ford's, held them with a gaze that was expressionless, gave nothing away. Perhaps there was an involuntary commendation for an officer who had succeeded in such a task before, grudging admiration. Or a reminder that past successes counted for nothing.

Anson's gaze moved on. If he had intended to make a point then he was satisfied that he had made it. At 44 he was ambitious, this was only a stepping stone; his sights were on a Chief Constable posting, maybe even Commissioner. If there was credit to be taken, he would take it. The one who killed organists offered a swift route to promotion.

Ford didn't go to the mess room afterwards with the rest of them. He would learn nothing there. Borman had given him a roving commission, it hadn't been rescinded; he had no specific instructions for Festival operations. He knew what he had to do and he would do it in his own way.

* * * * *

Michael Corms gleaned some consolation for the fact that he would not be the only organist playing in the cathedral during the Festival. His own role was almost a supporting one, a fill-in for routine services. The prime spot would go to John Weston of international fame for his midday concert on the Wednesday. Weston could be a coup, indeed, for some crazed killer obsessed with organists. Surely an assistant paled into insignificance beside such a big name.

He had not heard from Ford since the detective had called at the house that evening, Corms had hoped for some kind of confirmation of the promised security arrangements leading up to and throughout the Festival. There were plenty of uniformed police around the city, mostly to deal with the minority hooligan element, which most events attracted.

Corms had not noticed any police in the Close, possibly that area had been left to the plain clothes department. It wasn't very reassuring, particularly as he needed to practise in the cathedral during the evenings. He would not stop late, though; he needed to leave himself ample drinking time before the pubs closed.

"There's something different about you lately, San." He looked up from his plate, saw that she was washing up at the sink. "In fact, you've been a bit odd for the past few weeks, now that I come to think about it."

"Oh?" She said without even turning around. "I can't say that I'm aware that there's anything different about me.

Whatever do you mean?"

"You're … offhand, for want of a better word."

"Am I? If I am, then I'm surprised you've noticed it because you're never here."

"Nothing's changed in my routine lately."

"You're right there, it's been exactly the same ever since we've been married. You don't spend more than an hour a day in the house and at weekends you can always find something to do that doesn't involve the family. Not that I want you to stop going to the pub or anything like that, Michael." *For Christ's sake, I don't know how I'd cope if you started staying home!*

"It was just a thought; maybe I'm mistaken, I've got a lot on my mind lately. I'm going to have to start evening practices in the cathedral from tonight. Drinkwater's bringing the choir back in at seven, and after that I'll have to go through some pieces on my own."

"You won't be going to the pub, then?"

"Christ, yes, I want to be away by nine, back home to change and straight out. Just time enough to tuck the kids up before I go."

He had to get that bit in. Her lips tightened. It wouldn't be any different.

"Julie's hamster was dead when we got up this morning. Tears all round; we were late for school. I'll see if I can get her another tomorrow."

"Another rat to make a mess in the bedroom scattering its bedding all over the floor," he grunted.

"I hoover the mess up so it doesn't inconvenience you any, Michael."

"Isn't the dog good enough?"

"She wants a pet of her own, all children do. Ben's a family pet. And talking of Ben …" She glanced round to where the golden retriever was lying curled up on the mat. "He got out again this morning, through that same hole in the fence which you bodged up last Saturday. I had to go looking for him—he was in the deanery garden.

Fortunately, I don't think anybody noticed."

"Well, you'd better have a go at mending the fence yourself, you'd probably make a better job of it than me." He pushed his empty plate away, scraped his chair back, and stood up. "I'd better get back to the cathedral." He paused as a sudden thought struck him. "I got chatting to that writer fellow today, San."

"Oh, yes?" Sandra's heart flipped, she found herself clutching the edge of the draining board.

"Funny sort of bloke, I can't imagine why he wants to live in the Close. He was mooching in the cathedral, if you ask me he was doing some kind of research. Writes all this nasty stuff, so he told me. You know, blood and gore. Wouldn't surprise me if it was him that was mutilating the organists!" He laughed contemptuously. "Writing that sort of crap must affect the brain."

"What a horrible thing to say, Michael." She fought to keep herself under control.

"See you later." He made for the stairs.

"I'll probably be asleep in bed by the time you get home." she called after him.

Being asleep, or even feigning it, was preferable to resisting the advances of a drunken husband. Nowadays she felt guilty about sleeping in the same bed as Michael. It was as though she were being unfaithful to Gerry.

* * * * *

Michael Corms wondered why Homer was insistent upon taking the late shifts himself; apart from Needes and Lumby, there were other vergers. The Head Verger's role was virtually an administrative one, to delegate.

"Good evening, Mr Corms." Homer was like a cadaver, standing back in the gloom to allow the assistant organist to pass through the partly open north transept door. "I trust that the choir practice went well. Mr Drinkwater informs me that it did."

"It was up to standard." Corms was uneasy about having the door locked after him, it gave him a trapped feeling, just the two of them imprisoned inside this eerie place. "You can leave me the key if you like, Homer, if you want to get off. I can drop it through your letter box when I leave."

"Oh, *no*, sir!" A stern reprimand that such a thought should even cross the other's mind. "My duty is to lock and unlock the door, admit or refuse entry depending upon who it is and not to leave the cathedral unattended until – 10:30."

"Of course." Corms wished that the other would not follow on his heels the way he did. Security had obviously been tightened up recently following Lumby's neglect on the night of Rupert Frame's murder. "I've a few pieces to go through. I want to be away around nine."

"Give me a call, sir. I shall be at the desk. I have ample paperwork to keep myself occupied."

Michael Corms was decidedly nervous tonight, more so than usual. Logically, he had no reason to be, he reminded himself. The cathedral was secure; there was a man on night duty. No unauthorised persons could gain entrance.

Unless they were already inside.

He didn't like the organ loft, never had; even before Frame's death it had been a disturbing place. So cold and inhospitable, the lighting over the organ in a huge place of semi-darkness and shadows gave one a sense of being watched. You could be seen without seeing.

He sat listening for a moment or two before he switched on the organ. Total silence, not even Homer's echoing footsteps; the Verger was probably already seated at his desk by the west doors, immersed in his paperwork. Corms listened for that familiar hollow cough, like a death rattle, a nervous habit of the other's unless he had a bronchial complaint. There was none.

Michael Corms consulted his schedule; they had already practised Handel's *I Know That My Redeemer Liveth* earlier, he ought to run through it again. Also Psalms 41-43, they would be needed for Choral evensong on the first day of the

Festival. Most of all he needed to work on Elgar's *Serenade for String Orchestra*; Rupert Frame would have played that on the third night, it wasn't an easy piece.

He had stepped into a dead man's shoes.

He wasn't playing well, he was aware of that. Homer would be listening with a critical ear, making comparisons. 'Herbert Poppleton was the greatest, you know, a legend in his own lifetime. Nobody will ever match him'.

Corms paused, listened to the strains of Elgar dying slowly away up in the roof. It was as if they had penetrated the cathedral spire, rumbled their way right up to the top and had become trapped there. It seemed an eternity before the silence returned. And still Homer did not walk or cough.

A noise. So faint that it was barely perceptible, like a scraping shuffle. Corms tensed, listened intently. It came again. Stopped. He trembled.

Perhaps it was a mouse—there were bound to be mice, even in the cathedral. He thought it came from the steps leading up to the organ loft, peered into the semi-darkness. It was impossible to see, the shadows played tricks with you, you thought that you saw something and then it melted away.

He didn't really *have* to practise late, yet he did. There was a lengthy choir practice tomorrow which would take up most of the morning, followed by a sung Eucharist. He had to get that Elgar piece right, and time was running out on him.

One note but the unidentified sound beat him to it; a split second before the organ music drowned it out, but it was enough to bring Corms up out of his seat. A mute cry of terror, cowering, his arms flung up to protect his head from whatever lurked in the darkness of the balcony.

It isn't your head he's after.

There *was* somebody there.

A silhouette that was neither a shadow nor in Corms's frightened imagination, a shape that stood back, saw him and watched him.

Homer? It *had* to be the Head Verger, because there was nobody else inside the cathedral and the doors were locked.

It wasn't Homer, because whoever stood there was too short, the shape was all wrong. And for Michael Corms that was a terrifying realisation. He might have fled, except that there was nowhere to flee; the stranger stood between himself and the steps, which led down to the nave. He would surely have cried out, maybe even screamed, had his voice been able to function.

Instead he just cringed, waited for the other to advance, a luckless rabbit mesmerised by a hunting stoat.

The shape moved from out from the shadows, stood on the fringe of the organ lights, visible only from the waist down. Jeans, well-worn but not frayed, off-white trainers that were slightly scuffed.

Corms reacted with an instinct which bypassed logical thinking, grabbed for the heavy music tome that stood on the stand, his shaking fingers lost their grip, the volume slid from his hand, fluttered like a shot bird and thudded to the floor. A cry of fear and frustration escaped his lips, he might even have screamed had not a familiar voice spoken from the darkness beyond the organ.

Those trainers moved forward, the light travelled upon the stocky body, past the waistband of the jeans, and onto a pale blue sweatshirt. On upwards as the figure came closer, the light showed a square jaw, rugged features, close-cropped dark hair.

Recognition. Corms's relief merged into anger, surprise that checked the sharp retort. The weakness had him sinking back into the organ seat.

"I'm terribly sorry if I startled you, Mr Corms," Ford said, and smiled what might have been a genuine apology.

14

Sandra had made up her mind that she couldn't wait four years to leave Michael. She awoke depressed on that sunny July morning when John Weston was scheduled to give his organ recital in the cathedral and the Close was already filling up with tourists, and made her decision. She would go round to Gerry's house later and break the news to him.

Her depression was a hangover from yesterday's fiasco with the washer-dryer. It had been leaking for weeks, a slow seepage which suddenly became a flood. She had phoned the engineer; he had called within a couple of hours and ten minutes later he was shaking his head in despair. The bearings would not fit tightly enough to stop the leak on the new drum. The repairs, had they been possible, would have amounted to around £150, the engineer had explained, and who was to say that the motor might not pack up next week.

"It's out of guarantee, you've had it three years," he mumbled with some embarrassment, consulting some documentation fastened to a clipboard.

Well, Michael would have to buy a new machine. He could write to the makers and lodge a complaint about a design fault also. He wouldn't, though, because he was too lazy. She bundled a pile of dirty washing into a bin liner; the launderette was the answer to the current problem. She checked her purse to make sure that she had enough money for the machines. Michael wouldn't pay; he would tell her to add it to the already increasing amount in her creditor's book. And that would be that.

The schools broke up for the summer holidays next week. That was an additional problem: her visits to Gerry would be curtailed. Phone calls would be restricted to after bedtime, and even then she would have to speak in a quiet voice.

"I've come to a decision, Gerry." She put the kettle on, saw that there was a completed typescript in an envelope on the table. Officially, it was her job to check it for typos. She enjoyed reading his work—not that she was a horror fan, it was just that anything to do with Gerald Norman was exciting.

"To send the kids away to the grandparents' for the summer holidays." He was in one of his annoying flippant moods.

"Ha, ha, very funny." She wasn't in the right frame of mind for his humour. "No, nothing to do with the kids … well, yes, it is, really. Very much so."

"Go on then, spit it out." He seemed suddenly uneasy.

"Gerry, I … I don't want to wait four years for us to get together. I've been thinking about it, I'm just wasting four years of my life. Why should I have to put up with *him* for a day longer than I need to? I'd like us to go as soon as possible."

"I would, too." He nodded.

She stared. Maybe she had expected excuses, an expression of dismay, but she detected relief in his smile. "Gerry … are you sure?"

"Absolutely." He stared into his mug as though suddenly it was the most important thing in the world to him. "I didn't really think you'd stick it out for another four years, I was just waiting for something to happen, and obviously it has."

"It was after four this morning when Michael came home. He was very drunk, the worst I've ever known him. He's gone to the cathedral with a monster of a hangover this morning." She declined to add that the washer-dryer breakdown had been the flashpoint, the proverbial last straw. It sounded trite.

"Why'd he hit the booze like that?"

"I don't know exactly, but something scared him like I've never known him scared before. He came back from the cathedral, he'd been practising late last evening, and he was white and shaking. He said it was nothing, but something had happened."

"Maybe he thought he saw a spook."

"This killer, more like. Anyway ..." Sandra admitted to herself that that was the reason she had to get away, take the kids with her. It was selfish, she wasn't thinking of her husband. "I want to leave Michael, and I want you to leave Jane, Gerry."

"All right."

"When?"

He opened a folder, consulted something scrawled on a sheet of loose-leaf. "Mid-January, love."

"Mid-*January*!"

"Why, what's the problem? Only last week it was four years, now we've cut it to six months and you're obviously not happy with that."

"I can't stick another six months, Gerry!" She was pleading now, close to tears. "I'll go right round the twist."

"First," he leaned his elbows on the table, placed his fingertips together and pursed his lips, "we have to find somewhere to go. Unless we do that, then the only alternative is an old van and joining these New Age travellers!"

"I wish you wouldn't joke about it."

"I'm not, I just want to make it plain that we have to have a plan."

"Michael always says you have to have a plan."

"For once he's right. I have to find somewhere for us to live, work out the finances."

"What about your wife?"

"I'll handle that. What about Michael? Darling, it'll take weeks, maybe months, to get everything organised."

"I don't see how you're going to be able to afford to keep two families."

"Now it's you who is creating obstacles."

"Gerry, why don't we just pack up and *go*?"

He sighed. "Darling, it isn't quite as simple as that. I said January because I can have my next book finished by then, we have to have money to live on. Also, I need a break in my work schedule to be able to sort out the move."

"You're sure you're not just stalling me?"

"Christ, no!" He stood up, walked to the window. "I love you, I can't envisage life without you."

"All right. I hear Michael's been talking to you."

"I met him in the cathedral."

"What were *you* doing in there, Gerry?"

"I was doing some research for a book and I just happened to bump into him. Why, does it matter?"

"Not really."

"It obviously does by your tone of voice."

"I don't like the cathedral, it frightens me. I don't like you going in there, Gerry."

"In case this nutter carves me up? I can assure you he only kills organists."

"And assistants?"

"That's not a very nice thing to say, I wouldn't even wish that on your bastard of a husband, Sandra."

"The police are watching everybody who goes into the cathedral. There's closed circuit TV cameras everywhere, like they have in the supermarkets to trap shoplifters. That was how Adrian Frame got caught a few months back."

"So what?"

"They'll have you on film, Gerry, they might even come and interrogate you."

"I doubt it, but at worst they'll only waste valuable writing time."

"I suppose so."

Anybody who was remotely connected with the cathedral and its Close frightened her. It was a place of violent death. The killer might be somebody she knew.

She wished fervently that Gerry had not gone there.

15

This year's Festival had been the best ever, according to *The Mercury*, since its launch in 1982. Ford read the lengthy review carefully; there was little that he did not already know, he was unlikely to turn up anything of relevance to the case, but he was methodical. He needed an overall picture in his mind; the cuttings would be consigned to his already bulky file.

He read and studied the review of each event, beginning with the opening lecture on the science and sounds of music by an eminent professor in the Civic Hall.

The choristers had excelled themselves later that same day with a programme that included Handel and Psalm 23. Michael Corms was commended for his organ playing; Ford recalled that recital: the detective had been seated in the rear pew, he had spent the time studying every member of the congregation, poised like a coiled spring should anything happen. Frame's widow had been there; at one stage she had hidden her face in her hands. Her eyes were red rimmed afterwards. James Drinkwater had led the singing impeccably.

Choral evensong had been routine; without his constant vigilance Ford would have been bored. Strangely, Charles Homer was seen little during these services as he had delegated the duties, mostly to Lumby and Needes.

The orchestral recitals were less of a mental strain on Ford; nothing amiss was likely when there was no organist. All the same, he did not relax, he never took chances.

He did not concern himself with lectures; he left the security to constables, but he did, reluctantly, admit to enjoying *The Marriage of Figaro*. He was not musically inclined; on the few occasions when he sang with the cassette player in the car, he changed key on innumerable occasions. He only sang when he was alone.

John Weston's organ recital was the climax to Ford's

feeling of rising tension. He watched and waited, it seemed an eternity. Weston, the famous organist was unaware that he was under police protection by a CID officer posing as a hotel maintenance man who was on duty outside the room door throughout the nocturnal hours.

But there was no cause for concern. Weston left the city early the next morning.

One of the world's leading early music ensembles with a wide repertoire of medieval, renaissance, and baroque music performed in the cathedral on the following evening, followed by a piano recital in the Lady Chapel.

Choral evensong was daily at 5.30pm. Ford found it repetitive and boring, and he had to struggle to maintain his concentration. Each evening he followed Michael Corms home; he did not consider it necessary to accompany him on his nightly drinking sessions. On those occasions when Corms used his car, the detective felt that it would have been condoning drink driving. Corms had been lucky on both counts. So far. The killer might not get him, probably considered him to be an inferior victim in terms of status, but for sure, by the law of averages, the police patrol cars would stop him and breathalyse him one night.

Ford would have no sympathy when that happened.

There were musical performances most days in the cathedral, few of them included an organ accompaniment; a brass quintet and wind quintet, pride of place going to the City of Birmingham Symphony Orchestra. A production of *The Phantom of the Opera* filled every available seat, both aisles lined with chairs to accommodate the fully subscribed audience.

A brass band played on Stowe Fields on the Saturday night. Fortunately, the fine weather held. This was followed by the annual grand spectacular firework display to conclude the Festival.

Ford had given a tempered sigh of relief as he left the field, jostled with the crowd after the finale. The Festival had been hard work for the force—ten days and nights of climbing tension, long boring hours spent on fruitless vigils.

"Maybe you can relax for a while now, love." Brenda came through from the kitchen carrying a mug of tea. "You did your job and nothing went wrong. That's what policing is all about. VIPs that have to be escorted to and from public appearances, armed units and helicopters following them, everybody hopes that nothing will happen. When it doesn't, you feel it's all a waste of police time. But without police protection, some guy might have died. Look upon it as preventative action: the police presence in and around the cathedral kept the killer from making an attempt. You won."

"No." Jason Ford smiled wryly. "We didn't win, the bastard's been laughing at us all the time. He's run up a bill of tens of thousands of pounds for the taxpayer, he's had every cop in the city scrutinising faces until their eyes hurt. And he never *intended* to make a move—it's all been a game for him. The press have hyped it, made Jack the Ripper seem like a fond uncle by comparison."

Brenda Ford nodded, she understood only too well.

"Now he hopes we'll relax the security." Ford walked across to the window, stood looking out across the open plan estate, rows of identical houses with neatly mown lawns, cars parked in the driveways. A comfortable and safe existence for nine-to-fivers; all they had to worry about was their mortgages. Nobody would stalk them or kill them because they weren't interesting enough.

"You think he might strike again, Jason?"

"No doubt about it." When Ford turned round, his smile was gone. "He won't stop now, they never do. He'll kill, and kill again, until he's caught. That's the only way he'll ever be stopped. The Festival was his bit of fun, he revelled in the publicity. Somewhere in the teeming masses of this city, he's been laughing at us. Now the laughing's done, and this is where we get down to serious business."

She said, "I know," and because she knew she worried for her husband's safety.

"The chief's recalled most of the extra men to routine

duties, something that would never have happened in Dawson's day. Just a handful of us are left on the case. Maybe the killer's waiting for a new organist to be appointed; he doesn't get a kick out of mutilating a stand-in. The job has suddenly become the hot seat, I don't reckon there's going to be the usual flood of applicants. We're playing a waiting game; once there's a full time organist in the cathedral again, that's when this guy'll creep out of the woodwork. In the meantime, we don't stand a cat in hell's chance of finding him, but we have to keep looking."

PART TWO - AUTUMN

16

"I *hate* my father!" Adrian Frame screamed from the landing, banging on the banisters with clenched fists, vibrating the solid oak structure right the way down to the hallway below. "I hate him and I'm glad he's dead. I'm glad somebody …"

"Adrian, *please*!" Philippa Frame appeared in the kitchen doorway, tried to hold back her tears even though she could not stop trembling. "I won't have you speak of the dead, your own father, like this. Stop shouting—the entire Close will hear you and you'll be heard inside the cathedral."

"Good, I'm glad." The lanky youth, wearing a crumpled denim shirt and torn jeans, came slowly down the stairs, a step at a time. A deliberate, threatening advance. He spat, screwed his pallid acne-covered features up into a snarl. "Like I said, somebody did me a big favour; I just wish I'd done it myself."

His mother's instinct was to cower, maybe even flee, make a dash for the door, run outside. Lately she had become very frightened of her son. But he was still her son, and that was why she stood and faced him now.

"Your father did everything possible to help you, Adrian. You've no cause to hate him."

"Haven't I?" He descended another step, paused. "It was him that shopped me to the police when he found pot in my room."

"Because he loved you, Adrian."

"*Loved* me!"

"Yes, he wanted to stop you before it was too late, before you became addicted. It was the only way, we talked it over. We didn't do it lightly."

"You, too!" He hissed. "You cow!"

"It obviously didn't do any good." Philippa Frame had lost a stone in weight these last two months, and her only son wasn't allowing her to grieve in peace. "Now you're facing shoplifting and assault charges, and you're on crack, too. Just look what it's done to you, just go and see for yourself in the mirror. You're not the same person you were three months ago, either physically or mentally."

"And I'm glad," he laughed, a harsh sound, stepped down into the hall, "because that way I'm no longer his son. Nor yours. I'm *me*."

"You're in court next week." Her voice shook. *And pray to God that they send you for treatment. I just want to be left alone to grieve.* At least Rupert had been spared the shame, the ignominy.

"*If* I'm around." Adrian's eyes seemed to film over, his voice sounded far away like an echoing whisper in the silent cathedral across the road.

"What … what d'you mean by that?" She felt physically sick, held on to the carved dolphin table by the telephone for support. "You … you're not going anywhere, Adrian … are you?"

"I might be."

"You mustn't. If you don't turn up in court, they'll issue a warrant for your arrest. You'll be sent away. And fined. And now that your father's gone, I don't have the money to waste on fines. *Please*, don't cause me any more trouble."

"I'm going out." He moved unsteadily toward the door.

"*Where?*" She was always frightened when her son was away from home; if she had had the strength she would have barred his way, locked the door, and kept him prisoner in the house. As it was, her vision blurred, the room seemed to tilt, and she thought that she might faint. *Oh, Rupert, if only you were here.*

"It's my business where I go." He tugged the door open, turned back to face her. "But if you're really worried, Mother, I'm going into the cathedral. Don't you like the idea? The house of God, Father's shrine of worship, the place where he spent the most of his dreary, hypocritical life. That's where I'm going."

"I don't want you to go in the cathedral, Adrian."

"Oh?" His eyebrows lifted in mock surprise. "Why ever not?"

"Because … because …" Her pallid, hollowed cheeks flushed, the tears that misted her eyes began to roll. "Because your father's memory should be left in peace."

"You mean people will see me, associate me with him, think that maybe when he was younger he was like me." He spat on the floor. "I expect he was. Do you know what organists and choirmasters are notorious for, Mother? You don't? Well, I'll tell you, then. They interfere with young choirboys."

"*Adrian, how dare you!*"

"Well, it's true, if you believe what you read. You want to live in the real world, Mother, read the papers. The proper ones, the ones that tell you what goes on in this sordid life that's camouflaged by do-gooders. Only last week a vicar was put away for doing naughty things with little boys. Five years he got; it should have been ten. Just think about it, think what somebody did to old Poppleton, and to your husband, my father. Somebody got their revenge for …"

"*Shut up!*" Philippa screamed, on the verge of hysteria. "Your father would never dream of doing such things."

"That's what all wives and mothers say until it's proved otherwise." Adrian began closing the door behind him. "You mark my words, Mother, and remember what I said when the truth comes out!"

The door slammed shut and Philippa Frame sank down into the hall chair, buried her face in her hands, and wept openly.

* * * * *

Dick Lumby stood in the vestibule just inside the west doors of the cathedral, his huge frame drawn up to its full 6ft 2ins, his sombre Verger's uniform straining at the seams and buttons. He smiled to himself, lips drawn back from his protruding teeth, an expression of self-importance and smug satisfaction on his face.

This morning *he* was in charge. Of the entire cathedral. Everybody else was attending a meeting up at the deanery, something to do with new schedules for the coming winter. He didn't understand what it was all about, he probably wouldn't have been any the wiser had he gone along with the rest. Which was why he had been delegated the duty of verger-in-charge for the next few hours. The reason for his brief spell of authority was immaterial; he would bask in it whilst it lasted. Whatever the outcome of the assembly, Homer would write out his instructions in his own flowery and semi-illiterate hand and pin them up on the notice board. Dick Lumby would do as he was ordered; he would follow them to the letter; if one obeyed the guidelines laid down by the Head Verger that was a sure recipe for a peaceful existence.

He moved into the doorway, stood where he could be seen by the houses opposite, surveyed the blustery autumnal morning. Sunshine and squally showers, just like the weatherman on the television last night had predicted. A formation of black clouds had scurried on past the central spire, left in its wake concrete pathways glinting wetly in the aftermath of the heavy storm. Leaves blew, scattered in an easterly direction, piled up in any sheltered place that trapped them. Tomorrow, if the strong winds abated, a man with a barrow and broom, working at his own painfully slow pace, would continue his seemingly never ending task of sweeping them up. He never seemed to make much impression on the brown and golden carpet that littered the extensive lawns; there were still plenty of leaves left to fall from the lofty boughs of the horse chestnuts that lined the north side of the Close.

Lumby squinted through the thick lenses of his spectacles. Up by the schoolhouse in the corner of the Close some boys were poking amongst the leaves with sticks, hunting for conkers. It reminded him of his own boyhood, how he used to bake them in the oven until they were rock hard and …

Somebody was coming, a lone figure slouching down the wide slabbed walkway attracted his attention. He stiffened, his pulse raced. At least *somebody* would witness his brief moment of importance, seldom were there visitors in the cathedral before midday at this time of the year. By which time Homer—or his duly appointed deputy—would be here to officiate. Lumby checked that the flaps were outside his pockets, that his jacket was buttoned. He began to rehearse his welcoming smile.

He peered again. The on-comer was closer now, he could make out the hunched shoulders, those dragging feet scraping leaves in their wake, kicking them in a slovenly demonstration of his boredom and dissatisfaction with life itself.

Dick Lumby's smile faded, he sensed unease, apprehension. That figure was only too familiar with him; he didn't need to see the disagreeable features with their rash of spots. It was Adrian Frame, all right, undoubtedly heading for the cathedral. And that in itself was no small matter of concern.

The Verger's mouth had gone dry; he licked his lips in an attempt to moisten them. On a couple of recent occasions, the youth had mooched around the cathedral with an attitude of disinterest that bordered on contempt for his magnificent surroundings. He had stood for several minutes at the top of the nave staring fixedly up at the organ loft.

Perhaps he had been remembering his late father, paying a silent tribute, regretting the feud that had existed between them now that it was too late to make his peace. Until you caught a glimpse of the other's features: the staring eyes, lips clamped in a thin bloodless line. An expression of sheer malevolence, of drug-induced madness.

Homer had noticed it from his desk in the vestibule and, like a flitting ghoul, he had shadowed Adrian Frame until finally the other wandered back outside. It had been a disturbing experience.

"I don't want *him* in here," the Head Verger had told his subordinates at their weekly meeting. "He's up to something, I'll warrant. He's revelling in what happened to his father, and he's planning something. Vandalism, doubtless, possibly a desecration of the cathedral. He should be locked up for the safety of the public. He's dangerous. If he returns, request him to leave. If he refuses, call the police."

But how did one, especially a substitute Head Verger, deny a member of the community access to the cathedral? The doors were open to the public, entry was invited, encouraged because of the latest restoration appeal. A quarter of a million pounds was needed to repair the spires, every donation counted. Lumby fidgeted with his hands behind his back. Maybe—it was a desperate hope—the Frame boy wasn't actually coming inside, maybe he would stand and admire the statues of the kings that adorned the west facing architecture. Or perhaps slouch his way around the perimeter of the Close. No, he wasn't the type to take a morning constitutional.

The Verger stood with his powerful frame blocking the doorway, tried not to meet the hostile stare of the approaching youth. Lumby was physically strong, he weighed almost sixteen stones, he was a match for anybody; a teenage weakling stood no chance against his bulk. All the same, he trembled. Because the other's expression was one of sheer evil.

"'Scuse me." Adrian halted, his posture threatening. Possibly, had the other been of a slighter build, he would have attempted to barge his way past.

"Yes?" Lumby looked up. "Can I help you, sir?" He had a slight impediment of speech caused by his uneven teeth.

"You can get out of the bleedin' way, for starters!" Adrian's white and bony fists clenched. "I'm going in there."

Involuntarily, Dick Lumby stepped to one side, despised himself for his cowardice. He swallowed, his Adam's apple bobbed up and back down again. "Sorry." He dribbled, wiped the string of saliva away with his hand, hated himself for apologising.

But the other had already pushed past him, gone on inside, his trainers slapping the floor like wet plaice on a fishmonger's slab, echoing up to the roof. Adrian glanced contemptuously in the direction of the offertory table, headed on down the nave.

Lumby watched from a distance, knew that the Frame boy was going to stand and stare up at the organ loft the way he had done on his previous visit, a maniacal expression of hate for his dead father on his acne-infested features. Well, there was no real harm in that so long as he was gone by the time Homer returned from the meeting. Nobody need ever know that he had been here.

The Verger returned to the doorway, continued watching the leaves blowing off the lawns; their rustling was soothing, a rippling sea of golden brown. But his ears were trained back inside the cathedral, listening apprehensively. Those slopping footsteps had ceased; there was only an ominous hush from within.

What was Adrian Frame doing, for Christ's sake? Lumby didn't want to go and find out; the other was an obnoxious character in every conceivable way, he would probably turn out a string of blasphemous obscenities at the Verger's appearance. The youth was both arrogant and abusive and he smelled strongly of stale sweat, he probably slept in the clothes he wore by day because he was too idle to get undressed for bed. Likewise, it was doubtful that he washed or bathed.

You'll have to go and look, it's your duty. You're in charge. Dick Lumby's pulse raced at the thought.

The other might be defacing something, wantonly vandalising some tomb or memorial. And the Gospels were still on display in the Chapter House …

The Verger had to wait for his poor eyesight to adjust to the gloom of the interior after the bright sunshine outside. He took off his glasses, wiped them with a grubby handkerchief, put them back on. Looked again.

There was no sign of Adrian Frame, no sound by which he could be located. Just an eerie, menacing silence.

Oh, hell, this could get Lumby into an awful lot of trouble should Homer return unexpectedly.

The Verger coughed meaningfully and the sound echoed, grew in magnitude before it died away. The silence surged softly back.

He crept forward, tried to walk on the balls of his feet, but there was no way his cumbersome form could move silently. His leather soles *clip-clopped*, sounded like castanets, grew in volume. He abandoned stealth; he had to check on the Gospels immediately.

"*My dad was a fornicating shit!*"

The words hit with the force of a physical blow. Almost threw him back. An enraged, hysterical scream came at him from all directions, rippling with maniacal laughter. He smelled his own sweat, felt it turn icy with terror. His bowels threatened to empty, his legs weakened beneath him.

His thick neck jerked one way, then another. Gloomy shadows that could have hidden somebody even in the daytime. Another peal of laughter.

The nave and the aisles were empty. Unless the one he sought hid behind a stone pillar. There was nobody in the choir stalls, either, unless they were crouching down out of sight.

"*I'm glad my dad's dead.*"

The roof space vibrated. *Dead … dead … dead.* Mocking laughter reached its peak, faded.

The ensuing silence was worst of all. Standing there in the nave, Lumby felt eyes boring into him. Mad orbs that burned with crazed hatred. His mouth gaped, his frightened eyes rested on the distant altar; he offered up a prayer for his own salvation, glanced heavenwards. And met the hate-crazed stare of Adrian Frame.

"My dad got what was coming to him and I'm glad!"

Lumby recoiled, his eyes bulged like air bubbles about to burst. Above him, visible from the waistband of his jean upwards, Adrian Frame stood on the balcony adjoining the organ loft. His features were scarcely recognisable except for that unmistakable mass of acne, a gargoyle come to life so that it might vent its malevolence on those who revered this house of God, an awesome thing slunk up to its lair, aloft and now standing at bay.

The organ lights were switched on, a soft glow that was a sinister background behind the drug maddened creature that mouthed blasphemies and whose stretched lips frothed spittle. An arm came aloft; something glinted in the twisted fingers. A length of steel, a blade that shimmered. A knife honed to razor sharpness.

"I can smell my father's blood!" The nostrils dilated, the clogged mucus bubbled. "As fresh as the day it was spilled, it will still stink a thousand years from now. A sacrifice to the memory of the innocents who suffered at his soiled hands, a memory to be savoured now that he's gone."

Lumby trembled visibly; he thought that he was going to throw up.

"Come on up and see for yourself. The bloodstains are still visible if you look hard enough. Come and look, and smell the stink of his vile blood!"

No!

"Come on!" The knife was thrust forward, pointed at the cowering man below.

Dick Lumby found that he could move. Where terror had petrified him, paralysed him, now it provided him with the impetus to turn away. He heaved and bile scorched his throat, dribbled from his lips. Those legs which had struggled to bear his bulk now gave him the impetus to turn away, to flee.

A lumbering gait, he bumped against a pew, somehow kept his balance. Heavy footsteps, the echoes pursuing him, he dared not look back. His heartbeat, the roaring in his ears, was deafening. In his mind he saw the other coming after him, wielding that knife, stinking not of stale body odours but of the blood of a mutilated man.

Thirsting for blood again.

It seemed an eternity before he reached the vestibule, Homer's partitioned office on his right. He looked for the Head Verger, prayed that the ghoulish figure might rise like an apparition from behind the desk. A man feared by all—even Adrian Frame would be afraid of him.

But there was no Charles Homer seated at his desk. Nobody at all. The cathedral was empty except for himself and the madman who craved another mutilation and murder.

Nobody reached out to grab Lumby, to haul him back. No blade sliced into his unprotected quivering body. He stumbled through the vestibule, almost collapsed in the doorway.

Then he was outside, staring fixedly at the wind-blown leaves, and the schoolboys in the distance still searching diligently for conkers. The sun was hidden behind the next formation of dark clouds; it was starting to rain again, heavy spots that danced on the concrete.

The boys abandoned their search, ran for cover. Only then did Dick Lumby start to scream but the gusting rainstorm whipped his shrieks away, carried them back through the open door and into the cathedral.

Nobody heard him except the youth who stood in the organ loft brandishing a knife and laughing insanely. For him, it was sweet music in his ears, for he knew now how his father had screamed before he died.

17

"Good morning." James Drinkwater's tone was flat and expressionless, far removed from his singing voice in the choir. A man who lacked self-confidence smiled weakly and averted his eyes, glanced down at his scuffed suede shoes.

"Oh, good morning, Mr Drinkwater." Sandra Corms held the door open. There was an expression of nervous curiosity in her expression. She wore black jeans and a hand knitted black and white sweater. Her usually immaculate dark hair was in need of brushing; delivering four children to school was a harrowing experience. She had been making the beds when the front doorbell rang.

"Not a nice morning." The Vicar Choral licked his lips nervously, looked at her, looked away again.

"It's certainly autumnal. Can I help you?" The question should not have been necessary, but she envisaged them standing there on the step making polite small talk for the next hour. It was draughty with the door open.

"Er …" It was as though the other had forgotten the purpose of his call. "I … I just called to congratulate Michael on his appointment as organist to the cathedral."

"He's not in, I'm afraid." The door edged an inch or two closer, framed her in the gap. "He's in a meeting at the deanery." Her forehead furrowed, Drinkwater should have known about the meeting even if he did not include an invitation to members of the choir. And, in any case, he could have conveyed his congratulations to Michael after Choral evensong later in the day.

"Oh, I see. Yes, I seem to remember somebody saying something about a meeting this morning."

"I'm not expecting him back till around midday or later. Depending upon whether or not he goes to the pub for a lunchtime drink." She eased back a little; the gap between the door and the lintel narrowed another couple of inches.

"Oh, dear," he sighed, "my memory never was much

good. I could have saved myself a walk and a soaking if I'd remembered about the meeting."

She saw how wet his showerproof macintosh was, the way even his wiry, tufted hair was plastered flat on his head. A bedraggled figure, downcast after a futile walk on a blustery morning. Possibly he had wanted to be the first to congratulate Michael, hence he had not waited for a later opportunity. Which was why she said, "Would you care to come in for a cup of tea?"

"That would be most welcome, provided it's not putting you to too much trouble." Drinkwater edged a little closer to the door.

"No trouble at all." It was an inconvenience—she had never liked early morning callers. Almost a slave to domestic routine, she liked to get the beds made and the dusting done before her day started. She had hoped that he would make an excuse to leave. He obviously had time on his hands. Now it was too late; he was inside the hall, a nervous, boring creature like the rest of those associated with the cathedral. He bored her already, and he was making her nervous, too.

"Perhaps Michael will be back soon." He followed her through to the kitchen, knew instantly that she would apologise for the dishes stacked in the sink and the crumbs on the scrubbed pine table.

"I doubt it." Her tone said that she hoped he would not return early. "You'll have to excuse the mess, I'm afraid, I've only just got the children off to school."

"That's fine." He shrugged himself out of his damp coat, hung it over a chair by the Rayburn.

She reached down a caddy of tea bags, poured boiling water into the teapot. That was when she realised just how devoid of conversation she was. Anybody else, even a casual acquaintance, she would have been giving them a detailed run-down of the morning's rush to school. Words would not come; she could not think of anything to say. She regretted having asked him inside but it was too late now.

"I run a bookshop, you know." He accepted a mug of

tea, set it down on the table beside him.

"I had heard." Christ, what else could you say?

"I carry a wide range to suit all tastes. You ought to come and have a browse sometime."

"I'm not a booky person." End of the conversation. She turned round, slopping her tea because her nervousness had suddenly changed up a gear. It was his eyes, the way she had caught him looking at her, an intensity that bordered on lust. No, it couldn't be, it was her imagination. In all probability, he was criticising her. What was it Michael had called her the other night after he came home from the pub? A fat old trollop. Her lips tightened with anger; maybe James Drinkwater was thinking those same words. "I have to go out in twenty minutes, I'm meeting my sister in town."

He nodded, took a drink of tea. "One of my regrets."

"What?" Insistent. Frightened.

"I always wanted a sister. I had two brothers. I probably still have, but I haven't heard from either for at least twenty years."

Again, words eluded her. She wished that the phone would ring, a diversion. If it did, she would make an excuse to leave now. But it didn't.

"You must get bored in the daytime, with Michael in the cathedral and the children at school." He had heard about her affair with that writer; he wondered if she would mention it.

"Yes." *Oh Jesus Christ, I meant 'no.'*

"Daytime is often boring for me, too, particularly at this time of year when there are few tourists in the city. Some days I don't get a single customer in the shop."

"Oh, I see."

"I'm pleased for your husband."

"I feel guilty about it; he wouldn't have got the job if it hadn't been for …" Her voice faded, she looked away.

"A terrible business." She knew that he was looking at her in that way again. This time his gaze was focused on her breasts. "I just hope they catch whoever did it."

"I hope so, too." She searched for an excuse that might enable her to leave right now, leave her tea undrunk on the table. No, not an emergency—that might mean one of the children. Michael didn't come into it.

"Do you go to the cathedral services?"

"No, never. I didn't even go during the Festival when Michael was playing." She added, "Because I have to stay with the kids after school."

She sensed him now, a force that came at her, goose pimpled her flesh like he was touching her up with those long bony fingers of his. Her mouth went dry as if he had just kissed her. There was another feeling that had her wanting to heave. No, not *that*! *Because I know what you're thinking, you dirty old …*

"What's that?" His heard jerked round in the direction of the window.

"What?" Any diversion was welcome.

"It sounds like a police car. Or an ambulance."

Now she heard it, sirens that wailed like demons risen from the Pit, a sound that grew in intensity, became deafening in the time it took to recognise them. The noise almost certainly belonged to one of the emergency services.

"Good God!" James Drinkwater was at the window, his back to her, staring out. "Now, what on earth's going on out there?"

Heavy rain spots slashed the windowpane, streaked the glass and reduced visibility. Sandra stood on the balls of her feet, trying to see over and past her visitor. No way was she going close to him.

"What is it?" she asked from a distance.

"Well …" He craned his neck, rubbed at a patch of condensation. "There's an ambulance pulled up by the chain link fencing. A police car. No, *two*. Come and look for yourself."

"No, just tell me."

"Uniformed officers, two with guns. A couple of plain clothes policemen. They're all heading towards the cathedral. Something must have happened in there."

"I have to be going, Mr Drinkwater."

"There's more police arriving now."

"Do you think you could watch from outside, please?"

"There's a crowd gathering, the police are ordering them to keep back."

"*Mr Drinkwater, I have to leave. Now!*"

"Oh, I'm sorry." He turned around and it was as if a film had glazed his eyes, that momentarily he had forgotten her presence in the room. "Of course, how rude of me. Yes, by all means, I'll go and join the crowd outside."

Sandra followed him out, slammed the door behind her. It was raining sharply and she had forgotten her coat, but no way was she going back indoors. In case he followed her.

She turned away, began to walk fast, fought the urge to run. Once she looked back to make sure that James Drinkwater wasn't following her. There was no sign of him; the growing crowd of people had swallowed him up.

She was frightened, terrified. Not of whatever was happening back there, armed police running into the cathedral that was no concern of hers. Her fear was of a man who had gained entry into her house on a trivial pretence and then committed an act of voyeurism with the most penetrating eyes she had ever looked into. It was as if they had X-ray properties, the ability not just to see through her clothes but into her mind. He had lusted for her, not just for her body but for her soul.

She slowed her pace, felt sick again. It was just like they had had intercourse; she had been mentally raped and her flesh felt dirty as a result.

It was with no small amount of relief that she mounted the steps up to Gerry Norman's front door and leaned on the bell.

Somewhere behind her a police hailer was ordering the crowd to move back.

18

Borman's expression said 'it's *him*' when the call came through. Aloud, he was a complete professional as he gave orders for an armed backup. The report said that a man with a knife was at bay in the cathedral but you never ruled out the possibility of a concealed gun. You didn't take chances.

He told them to pick up Ford on the way. For a lot of reasons. He wanted Ford to be in a the kill. As a spectator. He didn't want him taking any credit for this.

Ford could have drawn weaponry, but he didn't. It would be a talk-down job; it might be over in a few minutes, or it could take hours. There was no pattern to sieges.

It took them three minutes to reach the cathedral. The uniformed officers had already cleared the area in front of the west doors; a patrol car blocked the Dam Street end.

Ford stood back; this was no time to make his presence felt. An ambulance arrived, parked behind the police vehicles. Detective Inspector Finch used the hailer, signalled to a couple of constables to enforce his order to the swelling crowd to move back.

Several of the vergers were grouped outside the west doors. Ford noticed that Homer was in conversation with one of the canons. There was no sign of either bishop or dean; it wasn't their scene. This was bad press for the Church, they would need to play it down. Strangely, he felt sorry for them because it had come to this.

"We have to adopt a low profile." Borman walked across to where the armed unit stood waiting. "According to reports, the son of the murdered organist has gone crazy. He has a history of drugs." *So don't look for normal reactions*, Ford thought. "As far as we can ascertain, he only has a knife. Inspector Finch will negotiate with him. Right, let's go in."

Ford brought up the rear, wished for a lot of reasons Borman hadn't called him in on this. In a way he was the fall guy. We just want you to watch us succeed where you failed, Ford. You've been on the investigation three months and you haven't come up with anything constructive. In the end, we had to do your job for you.

It's him—we're going to make sure it is. Just like Dawson did in the old days. Get me a confession and a conviction. Chief Dawson got his kicks from closing files; Borman was emulating him. You built up a formidable track record and you got a top job. It all came down to ambition in the end.

There were eight of them in the cathedral, Ford did a head count; Borman and Finch, two armed officers, two uniformed, Sergeant Clifford, and himself. He knew he didn't figure in the operation; he had been brought along as a scapegoat. They'd work it that way: if anything was to go wrong, blame DS Ford.

The lighting was full on, but there were still dark corners and shadows. The sculptured head of a long dead bishop followed their progress with stone eyes. You have entered the House of God.

The echoes went to work on their footsteps, simulated a funeral march. Somebody's going to die; it could be any one of you.

Ford saw that Mike Clifford nodded, a barely perceptible bow to the altar beyond the choir stalls; the DS was a religious man, they shouldn't have brought him along.

They halted, waited for the echoes to fade. Ford sensed the uneasiness that every one of them felt, even DCI Borman. They had entered a sacred place, they would violate its sanctity if they had to. There had already been one violent death here, up in that organ loft.

Their eyes were uplifted; they followed the balcony along to where the organ pipes stood like outdated ack-ack barrels trained vertically in anticipation of a Luftwaffe raid. So sinister in the half-light.

There was nobody in sight up there.

Finch cleared his throat, it rasped up in the rafters. He

was still clutching the hailer, glanced almost foolishly at it. He wouldn't need it in here; a whisper was good enough.

The armed officers had their pistols trained on the organ loft, .38s, left hands gripping right wrists, stoic expressions. Automatons of the law.

Waiting.

"Police!"

Finch's echo came back. "*Ple … ease.*"

No movement, no sound from up there.

"Throw down your knife and walk slowly down the steps, arms raised!"

No answer.

The marksmen were synonymous with the statues in the aisles, Ford had the unreal feeling that they would stay there forever if nobody ordered them to move. The stone bishop watched intently, maybe he prayed.

Borman was uneasy, fidgeted with his fingers. Far rather would he have faced abuse; threats had a positive situation. There wasn't anybody up there; the Frame boy had run off whilst Lumby was raising the alarm. He could be hiding anywhere in here. Or outside. He would have been very foolish to remain up there in the organ loft. They had to be sure, though.

"Show yourself. Thrown down your knife and come down."

Down … down … down …

Somebody was going to have to go up there. It would be one of the marksmen, the other covering him; Ford knew that they wouldn't let him go. *You're* only here to watch.

Behind them a door banged, echoed woodenly. Even from that distance they felt the gust of autumnal wind. Six heads turned; the marksmen might not have heard, there was not so much as a flicker of those steely eyes that remained trained aloft.

A woman's voice, verging on hysteria. "Let go of me! My boy—what have you done to my boy?"

Homer held Philippa Frame by the wrist in a beauty and

the beast struggle. Desperation lent strength to the kick that brought a grunt from his lips, made him relax his grip. It was enough for her to pull free, then she was running, panic on her features, fleeing down the nave. A uniformed constable made as if to pursue her, changed his mind. Beyond the vestibule was CID territory.

It was Ford who caught her, a grip that was both strong and gentle. Sympathetic.

"You can't go up there, Mrs Frame. We're not sure that Adrian's up there, anyway." Words that succeeded where force might have failed. He felt her sag against him, heard her begin to sob.

Still the armed officers did not glance round.

She shrieked, "He didn't do it, I know he didn't!"

"*I know he did …*"

Liar! The echoed mocked accusingly from up above.

"Adrian wouldn't kill his own father!" she yelled back at them.

"*Kill his own father …*"

Everybody was waiting again.

"Show yourself!" Finch's impatience came through. "Just let us *see* you!" *For Christ's sake.*

The marksmen appeared to tense. A psychic's challenge to the unseen: you might see it, you might not.

Ford wondered how long the cathedral had been left unsupervised between Lumby's terrified exit and the arrival of the vergers. A minute would have been long enough for Adrian Frame to run down the steps and hide elsewhere. Or flee outside. He could be anywhere by now.

There was no longer anybody up there. It figured.

Borman continued to fidget, bumped the hailer rhythmically against his thigh, he should have remembered to leave it back in the car. Sergeant Mike Clifford traced a wet tongue along dry lips. If the marksmen's arms were tiring, they showed no outward sign of fatigue, not so much as a sideways slip of their eyeballs to check on the chief.

Sooner or later somebody had to go up there. Sooner

rather than later.

Ford felt how Philippa Frame shook, a build-up of grief and despair that would have to erupt. Sooner or later.

Her damp hand clasped his own, she was holding on to him, she no longer needed his restraining grip. He tried to see her face but her head was bowed. The uniformed police and the vergers stood in a huddle at the end of the nave. Everybody was just watching.

Everybody was watching everybody else.

Borman said flatly, "We'd better go on up."

One of the armed officers lowered his pistol; if he felt relief, not a flicker of an eyelid revealed it.

There was another moment of waiting and watching one another, and that was when Philippa Frame tore herself free of Ford, moving with a speed that belied her slumped posture, deceived them all. A sorrowing, stooped woman was transformed into an unbelievable athlete; with a swivel and a bound, she took the steps up to the balcony two at a time.

"Stop her!" There was a ring of futility to Borman's shout; he could have caught her as she passed him, pulled her back. Instead he looked to the armed officers, Finch, Clifford, and finally to Ford.

Ford moved ahead of them all, but by the time he gained the bottom step, Philippa was at the top. She turned just once to look back, and then she was lost from view.

Ford did not hurry—there was no point. There was nobody up there for her to find, no wayward son brandishing a knife and cursing his dead father.

Nobody at all.

The scream rent the silence, was magnified all the way up to the roof, seemed to vibrate the architecture. The watching statues seemed to shake with rage at this sudden sacrilege. The vergers at the end of the nave huddled closer; there was safety in numbers.

Ford was halfway up the steps when he saw the figure rise up from behind the balustrade of the organ loft; blood smeared features that were crunched into an expression of shock and disbelief. A female face was barely recognisable as that belonging to Philippa Frame. Her mouth was shaping up for a second scream but her vocal chords were powerless to release it. Trying to force it, arms beating the air, fingers dripping blood and sprinkling it in all directions, spotting the organ pipes scarlet, splashing the watchers below.

It seemed an aeon before she finally got the scream out.

Ford didn't make it to the top. Philippa Frame met him two steps down, barred his way; there was no room to pass. She was holding on to the sides, barely capable of remaining upright. She swayed. Any second she would collapse.

She was mouthing incoherently, quivering, distraught words. A hand went to her mouth, came away again, left bloody finger marks on her face.

"My boy." Her eyes were closed; her lips were streaked with blood. Her hands were held aloft, her slippery, scarlet fingers told their own tale. Somehow she still stood, defying Ford and those below who were crowding onto the steps.

Ford stretched out a supporting hand. She ignored it, bared her teeth at him. A fist clenched, but she had not the strength to use it.

"*They* did this to him." A depreciative wave that incorporated the interior of the cathedral, the Close, the watchers below. "All of them, all of you. He was hounded so that in the end he turned on himself in the same way that somebody turned on his father. *Oh my God, he's done it to himself!*"

Ford's reactions were fast enough to catch her as she fell.

19

Ford had no official reason for calling on Cecil Clay now. In fact, the chief would doubtless go ape shit if he found out.

The file wasn't officially closed; at least, not until after the coroner's report was received. It was doubtful whether it would ever be proven that Adrian Frame had killed both his father and Poppleton. For the moment the incident room would be manned by just one uniformed officer. No calls had been received since the suicide. Everything would gradually be wound down, an unsatisfactory outcome. It was one of those untidy investigations, from here on it did not warrant manpower.

Ford's hunch, that nagging feeling that everybody was going for the obvious, had not gone away. The chief had his scapegoat, dead men unable to protest their innocence. Anson wanted the case closed, another statistic in his favour; he wouldn't thank anybody for trying to reopen it. From now on Ford must play it carefully, in his own time, adopt a low profile. The repercussions could find him back in uniform if anything went wrong.

"This *is* a surprise, Officer," Clay answered the door after a lengthy delay. Ford might have given up and gone away except that his acute hearing had detected movements somewhere in the bungalow. The other wore a plaid bathrobe over blue and white striped pyjamas, his wet hair lay uncharacteristically flat on his head. He had either been bathing or showering.

"I'm sorry if I've called at an inconvenient moment." The detective stood his ground. Possibly the other was expecting him to leave, return another time. You didn't play it that way; it gave the opposition breathing space, time to rethink. It was always a bonus to catch people wrong footed.

"Oh, no, not at all," embarrassment, a pursing of the lips. "Would you care to come inside?"

"Thank you." Ford stepped into the small hallway, detected that unmistakable smell of a bachelor abode; a lingering staleness, cooking smells that permeated the bungalow, air-freshener sprayed in an attempt to mask that nauseating aroma.

"Coffee?"

"Please." Hospitality was always a delay tactic, you exploited it.

"I've only got instant, I'm afraid. The percolator's broken."

"That's fine." Ford watched the other busying himself filling the kettle in the kitchen sink. Clay was clearly ill at ease. He spilled some coffee granules on the working surface, swept them up with his hands.

The detective's gaze roved the lounge, came to rest on the picture hanging above the fireplace. A rear view of a naked girl. There was nothing unusual in that; nude artwork was in vogue.

The frame hung silently off centre; the glass was spotted with drops of water like the outside of a window pain after a rain shower. Ford was puzzled; oil paintings were rarely framed behind glass. It looked odd. Maybe Clay had put it in the glass himself for some reason. To protect it from the damp? How did it come to be splashed in this dry centrally heated room?

"Sugar?"

"No thanks, just a splash of milk."

Clay came through, the mugs seemed to weight him forward, arced his spine. He stumbled awkwardly, slopped some of the dark brown liquid. "You've got your man, then, Sergeant. Or, rather, somebody has. I read in *The Mercury* that he did to himself what …"

"We don't have any conclusive evidence that the killer was Adrian Frame. Just a similarity between the mutilations and the mode of suicide, that's all. Maybe we won't ever know for sure."

"Oh, I see …" The other's expression changed, he

appeared to have become paralysed in the act of setting the drinks down on the low coffee table.

"A nice piece of artwork." Ford was staring at the picture over the mantelshelf. "Bought it recently?"

"Yes … I … um … er … purchased it from … from an exhibition in the … Arts Centre during the … Festival," Clay stammered, his cheeks suffused with blood so that a mass of freckles stood out starkly. His ears had turned a bright red.

"It looks like you've had it standing outside in the rain." Ford's remark was made to seem casual. He saw how the other stiffened, was trembling.

"Oh … oh, I see what you mean." Clay lurched over to the painting, rubbed at the droplets with his fingers, smeared the glass. "Dear me, how careless of me … I'd hung it in the bathroom, just somewhere to put it temporarily. I've only just brought it downstairs, you see."

"It's a nice picture. It must have set you back a bit."

"I … er …" Clay was vigorously lathering his hands with non-existent soap. "A few pounds, I can't remember exactly how much."

"It's erotic if you look at it long enough. A turn-on. Don't you think so?"

The other's blush was even deeper now. "I … I … I never thought of it in that way, Sergeant, but now that you mention it … yes, I suppose it could be … if you're that way inclined."

"You were a choirboy, weren't you?" A sudden direct question, fired without warning.

"Yes." A swallowed admission.

"In Poppleton's time, obviously." A statement.

Cecil Clay nodded; he was visibly shaken. He glanced back at the picture on the wall. The droplets of water had trickled to the bottom of the frame. A drip splashed onto the carpet.

"You used to go round to his place for tea and scones sometimes."

Another nod, the other's Adam's apple bobbled. His blush had gone, the freckles had faded, his complexion had paled.

"Did … anything ever happen?"

"I … I'm not sure what you mean, Sergeant." Clay sank down into an armchair, averted his eyes.

"I mean were you ever … *interfered with*?"

Silence. Cecil Clay's hands went up to his face, hid it. His head was bowed, he leaned forward. A shudder, it might have been a sob of despair. Of guilt. The whispered "yes" was superfluous.

"I see." A long silence during which Ford watched the other fidget, shift his feet, writhe inwardly. Clay looked out from between splayed fingers, closed the gap.

"I needed to know, Mr Clay." Ford's tone was apologetic. "I'm sorry if I've distressed you. It would have helped, though, if you'd told me before. I suspected as much. You see, I need to form a profile of Herbert Poppleton. I need to know as much about him as his killer. There has to be a reason why he was killed, why Rupert Frame was killed."

"It wouldn't have made any difference, would it?" Clay looked up. "I mean, the killer's dead, isn't he? Poppleton wouldn't have done anything to the boy, Adrian wasn't born in those days, and anyway, Frame wouldn't have been abusing his own son, would he?"

"He could have been. It happens. Frequently. But I, personally, don't believe that Adrian Frame murdered his father or Herbert Poppleton. Everybody has jumped to a convenient conclusion. All Adrian did was top himself in a bizarre copycat suicide. Maybe it was a crack-crazed final revenge on the father he hated, or even a twisted tribute to the real killer. We don't know. I mean to find out the truth."

Clay's head jerked up and he stared; for a moment speech was beyond him.

"Would you care to tell me about it? I'd be most grateful and I promise you complete confidentiality and anonymity."

"All right." Clay grabbed for his coffee, spilled some as he gulped it, oblivious of the stain on his bathrobe. "There really isn't much to tell, though, I'm afraid. Poppleton used to invite us round to his house from time to time. His wife was always absent, upstairs resting, I think. It was a strange informal—yet at the same time impersonal—meeting. Frightening, because you knew what was coming and you daren't refuse. Nor tell anybody." He reached for his coffee again.

"Go on."

"Always compliments, you were made to feel that you were the best in the choir, that he relied on you totally. Then … then …" Clay hid his face, spoke through his fingers. "Then he'd move across, sit beside you on the settee, and he'd say … he'd say …"

"Yes?"

"He'd say …" The words were barely audible. He closed his eyes and it seemed for a moment that he was about to faint, slump back unconscious into the chair, spare himself the shame and ignominy of his reminiscences. "He'd say, ' Shall we now sing Psalm 151?' "

Ford's eyebrows raised, he did not speak.

"You understand, Sergeant?" A fluster of embarrassment, like somebody who had told a lengthy joke but his audience had missed the point. Explaining would be an anticlimax; the only laugh would be at the expense of the teller.

"I'm sorry, I'm afraid you've lost me."

"Of course, it was silly of me to expect you to understand. You see … there are only one hundred and fifty psalms, the hundred and fifty first is non-existent."

Ford's forehead puckered, he waited.

"Psalm 151 was a signal that Herbert was … going to … to *do* things. I'd … I'd rather not go into details."

"Of course not." The detective stiffened. "I wouldn't dream of asking you to, you have been a tremendous help to me, Mr Clay. But, did these … *things* happen on a regular basis?"

"Infrequently. At least, as far as I was concerned. You must remember that there were eighteen choirboys." He paused. "So one's turn came round periodically. Sometimes, though, it was just tea and scones and a chat. I suppose it all depended on his mood."

"And the other boys—did you discuss it amongst yourselves?"

"Certainly *I* never told anybody, I was too ashamed. The memory has haunted me throughout my life … made me what I am, an insecure loner. I can never erase the feeling of guilt." He stared at the painting; the droplets had dried, left smears on the glass. "But Rupert Frame wouldn't have done anything like that. At least, I don't think so although I didn't know him. It was a long time ago. Charles Homer was a junior verger in those days."

"You knew Homer, then?"

"Yes, an unpleasant man, he toadied to old Herbert. If he knew you'd been up to something, he'd shop you to him. They used to say that Homer only got the job because of Poppleton, that they'd known each other somewhere previously. I can't for the life of me think why Poppleton befriended somebody like that. Homer used to go round to his house frequently, so it was rumoured."

"That's strange, indeed," Ford's eyes narrowed. He refrained from making a joke about Psalm 151, reminded himself of the old saying that there was many a true word spoken in jest. "I'll need to talk to some of the other choir members, Mr Clay." He rose to his feet. "Perhaps you might be able to furnish me with a list of names which I can try to trace. Nearly forty years is a long time."

"I …"

"Complete confidentiality," Ford promised and smiled reassuringly. "You have my word on that."

Cecil Clay slouched from the room in slippered feet, his body bowed. A few minutes later he returned clutching a blue cloth-bound booklet, tattered and dog-eared. "This should tell you all you need to know, Sergeant." He held it out. "A school register and diary of events for one of the years when I was a pupil. In the flyleaf is a list of choristers. I'm sorry I don't have any addresses. The only one that I've kept in touch with is James Drinkwater. I wish I could be more helpful."

"You've been more help than you'll ever know." The detective pocketed the booklet.

"You don't think Adrian Frame was the killer, then?" Clay's head was thrust forward as though the other's answer was of vast importance to him.

"I only have my own opinion." Ford shook his head; he wasn't prepared to explain his hunches. "I'll return your book in due course, I promise."

He cast one final sideways glance at the painting over the fireplace. For a brief second the girl seemed almost lifelike; he found himself tensing in anticipation of her turning around, smiling and unashamedly displaying the fullness of her nudity for his personal pleasure.

Which was why Cecil Clay had taken it up to the bathroom with him.

He pitied Clay for everything that he had undergone, the traumas of a disturbed boyhood that had spilled over into manhood. Whatever delights the girl afforded him, he deserved them.

20

"Just *when* are you going to do something *positive*?" Sandra had to restrain herself from shouting; anger and frustration had been building up inside her throughout a sleepless night. As soon as she had delivered the children to their respective schools she had gone straightaway to her lover's house. "I mean, we've talked and talked, promises and more promises, and we're no further forward than when we got together in the summer. July 17th, in case you'd forgotten the date," she added sarcastically.

"Look." Gerald Norman was visibly strained, the lines in his bearded face were etched deeply, he chewed hard on the stem of his pipe. "We've explored every possibility. You want a house, but right now I don't have the money to buy one. At my age I'd only get a ten-year mortgage, at most and there's no way I can afford that."

"What about this hoped-for bestseller that you finished last week?" She tapped the desk meaningfully.

"It'll take time, you know that. A moderate advance, the usual, and then we have to hope that it sells. Then we have to wait for royalties, six months after publication. Even with a blockbuster we wouldn't see any serious money for eighteen months."

"You do my head in," she sighed.

"You're always saying that."

"Well, it's true."

"All right." He spread his hands. "Let's just go take a chance. We'll probably live on the breadline, maybe under it. Okay?"

"I want security." She became sullen. "For the kids' sake."

"Fair enough, but you know the risks shacking up with a writer. It's a precarious way of making a living. But if you prefer, you can stay with Michael. You'll be unhappy and lonely, he won't give you a penny more than he absolutely has to, but you'll have a roof over your head and food on the table. You have to weigh whether that's worth putting up with what you've been putting up with for the last twelve years."

"You're a sod!" She smiled. "You know damned well what I'll choose. Michael married beneath him; I know damned well that's what his mother thinks. But I serve a purpose: I do his washing and cooking, bring up his kids, stay at home whilst he goes to the pub every night and …"

"And that, too?"

"Not anymore, I told you that."

"I want to give you everything I possibly can." His voice was husky, and for possibly the first time in forty years he was close to tears. "God, I do, San."

"I know." She sat down, her hand found his, squeezed it gently. "I'm sorry, Gerry, it's just that …"

"What?"

"I thought Michael was going, he was scared for his life, but now that the killer's dead, he's changed. He's been appointed cathedral organist, it's what he wants. So he's staying. Nothing has changed, life will go on as before, down to the pub every night, me left alone with the children. Bored and lonely, as you say. I can't stand it." She couldn't hold back her tears any longer. "I want to go *now*."

"All right." He put his arm around her. "I'll do something. I promise."

"I know." She buried her face against him. "I know you will, darling."

After a while he extricated himself gently. "I've got to pop out for a while."

"Shopping? I can get you anything you need."

"No, more complicated than that, I'm afraid. Research. I need to spend an hour or so in the cathedral."

"Oh!" She was surprised, alarmed. "Michael's in there, practising."

"So what?"

"It doesn't matter, I suppose." She was watching him

carefully. "It's just that he happened to mention on one of the few occasions when he found the time and the inclination to chat that you'd taken to going into the cathedral quite frequently lately."

"Because I'm setting a thriller in a cathedral setting." He laughed, but it sounded forced. "Anything wrong in that?"

"No, I suppose not. It'd give me the creeps to go in there again after what's happened, Gerry."

"At the back of your mind you think that just by seeing me around, and knowing that you do a bit of work for me, he might put two and two together."

"Michael would never suspect in a month of organ recitals," she sighed. "Not even if somebody told him. In fact, if I confessed, he'd call me a liar. He just wouldn't believe it possible, and neither would half the Close."

"The trouble with you, Sandra," he said, his expression serious now, "is that you've been made to feel like a second class citizen. From now on you're a person in your own right, you're important. To me. Get it?"

"I love you." She reached out for him again. "And Gerry …"

"What's worrying you now?" He sensed that she had been holding something back.

"Something else I have to tell you." She averted her eyes. "I should have told you a couple of weeks ago; I guess it isn't really important. It may never happen again, but it worries me all the same."

"Go on, tell me." He sat down again.

"Drinkwater, the Vicar Choral, he called round the morning after Michael's appointment was confirmed. He said he wanted to congratulate him, but he must've known that Michael was in a meeting in the deanery. Like a fool, I invited him in. He asked me to call in at the shop, said there were books there that might interest me. He was quite insistent; I found it rather scary. It was his eyes that frightened me most, like he could see right through my clothing." She shuddered at the memory. "That was the morning they found Adrian Frame dead. I was wondering how to get rid of Drinkwater when the police and ambulance arrived and it was the most welcome diversion I've ever known. I haven't heard from him since, maybe he's got the message that I don't want anything to do with him."

"He's a sly bastard." Gerry Norman's expression was angry. "I don't know him except to pass the time of day with, but I can believe what you say. An introvert, maybe a secret pervert, the same as that mate of his, Clay. There are rumours that Clay pinches girls' bottoms. If he comes round again, let me know."

"Thanks." She nodded. "I wasn't going to mention it to Michael; I didn't want to cause any trouble in the cathedral."

"I must go." He moved towards the door. "God, it's pouring rain again. Still, I'll be dry enough in the cathedral."

Sandra sat there staring at the door after he had gone. She didn't like him spending so much time in the cathedral. She shuddered, goose pimpled. For her, it was the most terrifying place on Earth.

She could not imagine why he needed to spend so much time in there.

* * * * *

Mark Millington was in his early fifties, slim and dapper with greying hair. He stood on the forecourt of his car sales plot and surveyed it with pride. A pair of Mercedes sedans gleamed in the wan autumn sunlight in an attempt to seduce a prospective buyer. Mark was proud of them, too; status symbols, you didn't need to drive them, you just stood beside them, basked in the envious glances of passers-by.

He has every reason to be proud of his achievements. Ten years ago this place had been a tatty three-pump filling station, the only building a shanty cigarettes and sweets kiosk. He had worked it alone, seven days a week, seven in the morning till ten at night, built it up to what it was now. His initial investment had been hard work and the determination to succeed. He had succeeded; last year his turnover was in excess of three million. Even the recession had not held him back; the secret was, he permitted himself a smug half smile, selling expensive cars to wealthy people. You didn't make anything out of old bangers, all you got were comebacks and refunds; the profit margin wasn't high enough on middle of the range cars, and those customers were the ones who suffered in a recession. But executives and professional people always had the money to buy what they wanted, regardless.

A movement caught his eye; somebody was crossing the road. A small, well-built man with short, dark hair. Millington eyed the other's attire; Mercedes customers often dressed casual, they didn't need to impress. But there was something about this guy that didn't slot him into that category. You could smell 'em when you'd been in the business long enough. Certainly not a rep, neither did he have the arrogance of bureaucracy. Somewhere in between. He gave up guessing and waited.

"Detective Sergeant Ford." The other's handshake was firm. "I wonder if you could spare me a few moments, Mr Millington?"

"Sure, come on into the office, Sergeant." The garage owner hid his disappointment; he would have liked to have sold another car before the end of the month to maintain the upward trend on the target graph on the wall. Still, there was another week to go yet. In all probability his visitor was investigating a car theft.

"How can I help you, Sergeant?" He sat down at his desk; it always gave one an advantage, like a headmaster interviewing a pupil about some minor misdemeanour.

"A long shot, really." Ford smiled disarmingly, knew only too well the psychological disadvantage in not being offered a seat. "Maybe no shot at all and I'm just chasing shadows. I believe you attended the Cathedral School in the late sixties?"

"You know more about me than I do." A preparatory

and public school education was Millington's vulnerability. It was a good background against which to sell high-class cars; it put him on an equal footing with his illustrious clients. It was something about which he liked to talk, but he never boasted. "How do you know that?" Curiosity prevailed.

"I've been lent a copy of the pupils' handbook." The slim volume was produced, held aloft. "Actually, I'm attempting to tidy up a few points in the Poppleton murder." *And for Christ's sake, don't go checking me out.*

"I thought the case was closed—the guy committed suicide."

"Like I said, I'm tidying up loose ends." It sounded vague. "We need a profile of the victims as well as the murderers. For the files. We use the information for future murders."

"I see. Jobs for the boys."

Ford didn't take the bait, he rode the jibe. "That's not up to me, I just obey orders."

"Okay." Millington leaned back in his chair, clasped his hands behind his head. "What is it you want to know, Sergeant?"

"Does Psalm 151 mean anything to you, Mr Millington?"

Millington jerked upright and his hands came away from his head. A momentary expression of shock before he regained his composure. There was only a slight tremor in his voice when he said, "So you've heard about that, eh?"

"Yes." Ford sat down without being invited to do so. And waited.

"Everybody knew about what went on." Millington was staring at a printout on his desk. "But nobody ever did anything about it. I think maybe even Wilson himself knew. But Herbert was a legend, a law unto himself. Unless a parent had complained—and to my knowledge none ever did—they were prepared to turn a blind eye to it, pretend that it never happened."

"You were in the choir yourself, Mr Millington?"

"That's right, and you want to know if Dirty Herbert ever did anything to me?"

"You don't have to tell me unless you want to."

"He tried once. I refused. Next term I wasn't in the choir anymore; Herbie claimed my voice had broken and that I was no longer any use to the choir."

"This is confidential." Ford leaned his elbows on the desk. "But do you know any boys he actually did do anything to? A name or two, perhaps?"

"It's been a long time." Millington pouted his lips in deep thought. "Christ, I can barely remember who was in the choir at the time."

"Run your eyes down this list, see if anything clicks." The detective pushed the open booklet across the desk.

"Now, let me see." The other held it at a distance, almost as though he was afraid to read the printed names. "Widdowson … God, he was a creep! And Elliott-Walsh, he went on to become Head Boy. I wonder what he's doing now …"

Ford watched, waited.

"Clay, he was weird. And Drinkwater—now Herbie took a liking to him, that much I can tell you. Whether there was anything between them, I wouldn't know. But Drinkwater went on to become Head Choirboy. Apart from that, I'm afraid I can't tell you much, Sergeant. It would be wrong of me to surmise."

"Of course." Ford took the register back, closed it, and slipped it into his pocket. "You remember Homer, doubtless?"

"Who could forget him?" An uneasy laugh. "Herbie's batman, we used to call him. Herbie got him the job, the Dean and Chapter didn't like him; we used to reckon that he only stayed because of Poppleton's protection. Why, for Christ's sake? He used to creep about the place like Frankenstein's monster resurrected, the boys were shit scared of him. I heard that he had a big row with Herbie over something and if Herbie hadn't been retiring, old Homer would have gone. But he's still there now. I went to one of the Festival performances in the cathedral and the old bugger doesn't look any different from when I was a boy. I'm sorry I can't be of more help to you, Sergeant."

"You've been a great help." Ford scraped his chair back as he stood up. "I'd appreciate it if you'd treat my visit as confidential, too."

"Naturally." Millington walked outside with him. "Myself, I'd say the Frame boy killed Herbie because the old boy was a representation of his father, then killed his old man because he hated him. Drugs are to blame, I'd like to see them bring in mandatory death penalty for drug peddling like they've got in Thailand. These drug barons are the real murderers; the addicts are just their pawns."

"Maybe." Ford made a dash for his car through the sudden rainstorm. In the distance, dark clouds were hovering over the cathedral spires. He shuddered involuntarily, a gut feeling that sent an icy trickle right the way up his spine and into the nape of his neck. Ominous. Like death had not deserted that holy place.

He reminded himself that if there was another murder then they were up against a serial killer. And serial killers didn't stop until they were caught.

21

Michael Corms had never been for a walk around Stowe Pool in all the time in which he had lived in the city. He had never had the slightest ambition to stroll the perimeter of the thirteen acres of water. Certainly not after dark on a rain-swept autumn evening.

He had not come here specifically. Indeed, he was scarcely aware that he stood on the cinder track atop the grassy banks, the wind rippling the surface and creating waves that lapped the stony shore.

He wore no topcoat, was dressed in the charcoal grey suit which he wore to the cathedral each day. He had not been home to change after Choral evensong. He had not been home at all. He wasn't sure whether he would ever go home again.

He stood there in the darkness of early evening, a stiff westerly wind billowing his jacket, flapping his tie. He had an urge to scream his anger into the night wind, to pour forth obscenities, to vent his uncontrolled rage on the elements.

He didn't.

He wanted to cry, his eyes burned with the dryness of sorrow.

The tears would not come.

He had just walked away from the cathedral aimlessly, head bowed, feet dragging. He had no destination in mind; he would just keep on walking until he collapsed with fatigue. He was not used to physical exercise, his leg muscles ached already and he was breathing hard. And the farthest he had come in that half hour was barely a quarter of a mile to where the old boathouse stood on the western shore of the lake.

He closed his eyes, clenched his fists so that his fingernails dug deeply into the palms of his hands. In some strange, masochistic way, the pain gave him relief from his mental agonies.

When he had played the final psalm, switched off the organ and its lights, he had been in a relaxed frame of mind. He had even considered walking into town for a quick pint at The Scales before going home.

Within a quarter of an hour he was a broken, totally disillusioned man.

He had even contemplated suicide. Not seriously, but the thought had been there. He considered drowning, walking out into the shelving pool until the water came above his head. But he knew that he would instinctively strike out and swim back to shore, however much he wanted to die.

He had a small penknife in his pocket; he could slash his wrists. Except that he did not have the courage, he had never been able to stand the sight of blood. Only alcohol had prevented him from having nightmares over Rupert Frame's murder.

An overdose of Paracetemol would have been painless, maybe even soothing. He had read somewhere that eight tablets were fatal. Only he didn't have any, and the chemist in town closed at five thirty. Which ruled *that* out.

Michael Corms accepted that he wasn't going to die. Not yet, anyway.

He hated his wife. Oh, Jesus Christ, how he hated Sandra! He hated Charles Homer even more; he wished that it had been somebody else who had told him. Because he wouldn't have believed anybody other than the Head Verger.

Michael had switched off the lights and was making his way toward the steps that led down from the organ loft when he became aware that somebody was standing in the shadows watching him. He started visibly, almost cried out loud.

"What the devil …"

"I'm sorry, Mr Corms, sir, did I startle you?"

"Yes, you did, Homer!" An angry retort, his voice

trembled with relief as much as fear when he identified the watcher on the balcony. "I do wish you wouldn't creep about like that."

"I'm sorry, sir, but I was always taught to tread quietly in the cathedral so as not to disturb others. A mark of respect, I'm sure you'll agree. I'm too set in my ways to change now, sir."

"I suppose so. Anyway, I've finished for the day, so you can lock the door behind me, Homer."

"Sir, I wonder if …" The other was uncharacteristically hesitant. "If I might have a word with you."

"Can't it wait until tomorrow?" The organist had already decided upon that pint of beer; temptation called him urgently, and he had no wish to delay his craving discussing petty cathedral matters.

"It has waited too long already, Mr Corms." There was a sinister, almost gloating ring to the other's voice. "And seeing as you have been appointed organist, I feel it is my duty to bring it to your attention, both in the interests of yourself, the Dean and Chapter, and the residents of the Close. Perhaps by informing you, I might be in time to avert a scandal that could be to the detriment of your position, sir. The cathedral has suffered enough already in recent months."

Michael Corm's heartbeat stepped up a gear; there was a sinking sensation in his stomach. "Scandal? What scandal?"

"May I have your promise that I might remain anonymous, that the information which I am about to pass on to you will not be linked with my name, sir?"

"Yes." A hoarse whisper. *For God's sake, say what you've got to say and let me get out of here!*

"I have agonized over telling you, sir. I hoped that perhaps somebody else would spare me the painful task but I can only conclude at this stage that nobody else knows about it. I pray to God that they don't, and that the matter may be sorted out privately and thereby prevent any vicious gossip."

"*Tell me*!" A shouted whisper.

"Very well, sir, but please understand that it is painful for me to tell you."

"Go on."

"Sir … I don't quite know how to put this, it is certain to be a terrible shock to you."

For a second, Michael Corms experienced a sensation of vertigo, as though he might fall from the balcony, plunge down the steps to the hard floor below. Instinctively, he clutched at the rail, hung on. "*For God's sake, what is it*?"

"It gives me great sadness to inform you," Homer paused, took a deep breath, his voice dropped to a scarcely audible whisper.

"*To inform you … inform … you …*"

Corms almost screamed at the echoes that threatened to drown the other's words.

"Your wife is having an adulterous affair."

Corms wanted to laugh; he managed to check his initial reaction. An expellation of pent-up breath that sounded vaguely like the organ pipes behind him. Then anger, but he managed to control that, too. Eventually, he said, "I beg your pardon?"

"You seem to have misunderstood me, sir, but I speak from my own observations. Your dear wife is seeing another man and I have reason to believe that sexual intercourse is taking place between them."

"That's crazy, it's a wicked lie. Sandra wouldn't …"

"I'm afraid that she already has, sir. I have reason to believe that it has been going on since before the Festival."

"Prove it!"

"*Prove … it … prove …*"

"That I can do, sir, if you wish me to."

"Who … who is this man?"

"A writer of scurrilous fiction, sir."

"Norman? No, that's impossible, he's married …"

"So is your wife, sir. Between them they have plotted deceit with unbelievable cunning. A job created for her, a smoke screen for their fornication."

"It's a lie!"

"Alas, I wish it was, sir, but unfortunately it is true. As I told you, intercourse has taken place, in the bedroom of Mr Norman's house."

"You can't possibly substantiate such a wild accusation."

"Indeed, I can, Mr Corms." Homer half turned, pointed towards the south transept. "Witness that small wooden door, sir, which is kept locked at all times. Only I carry the key. Behind it lies the staircase that leads up into the main spire and offers unsurpassed views of the city and its surrounding landscape. At intervals there are windows from which these views may be observed. One day in July, I happened to be up those stairs and I chanced a look out of a window. I assure you, sir, it was not my intent to look down upon the windows of the houses below. An accidental glimpse. The naked lady's face happened to be turned in my direction, and I could not help but recognise her as your wife. She was naked and enthusiastically engaged in the delights of extramarital sex. As was Mr Norman."

Michael Corms stared; his expression was no longer one of disbelief. He felt sick; he thought he might be.

"Far be it for me to spy upon such activities." The other's fingers entwined nervously. "But I considered it my duty to ascertain whether or not this was what is termed an 'affair'. I hasten to add that, on the afternoons of July 29th, August 4th, and August 7th, I again saw the said couple engaged in sexual activities. I am no voyeur; I merely looked quickly and came away. I made a note of the dates in my diary." He fumbled in a trouser pocket. "Of which I am happy to show you, should you wish to see them."

"No, I'll take your word for it, Homer." Michael's mouth was dry, but his thoughts were no longer on a pint of ale. *You shit bastard, you've just ruined my life!*

"If I can be of any further help to you, sir …"

Corms shook his head. *For God's sake, don't tell me anymore.* Gossip he would have scorned, maybe wild threats of an action for slander. Anybody else and he would have dismissed it as troublemaking tittle-tattle. Anybody … except Homer. Because Homer would have checked and double-checked, left no room for mistaken identity.

Sandra was having it off with that writer bloke, and the guy had had the cheek to walk around the cathedral most days lately. Doubtless the other was checking on the organist's whereabouts so that he could safely indulge in illicit sex with Michael's wife.

Corms staggered down the steps, lurched his way towards the north transept door. Numbed, he staggered out into the squally dusk, turned right at the top of the steps and headed blindly in the direction of Stowe Pool.

Now he stood there in the black shadow cast by the old boathouse. All around him the stormy night sky reflected the city lights, a kaleidoscope of colours. The wind brought with it the incessant sound of traffic, gusted it away again. People going about their business, oblivious to his own plight. They wouldn't care even if they knew. Nobody knew except himself. And Homer.

You bastard!

You bitch!

Never once had he thought of returning home and confronting Sandra. Because she wouldn't lie, and he would have preferred to hear lies and to believe them.

She had no reason to do it. Had she? He gave her enough money for her needs, anything over and above that would have been extravagant. The insurance had written off her car, soon they would come and take it away. She didn't *need* it; she could walk the children to school. The exercise would do her good.

It was a man's right to go out in the evenings and a wife's duty to remain home to mind the kids. She didn't have anything to complain about. She had a roof over her head, food on the table; even a television, and that was a luxury, not a need.

For Christ's sake, why had she done this? He gave her

sex. For a long time now she had been refusing it, so she hadn't wanted it. Sex was a husband's *right*, a wife's duty. She had shirked her duty, he had not complained unduly.

There was no reason for her adultery. He couldn't understand it, it didn't make sense.

He found himself sheltering from the wind behind the boathouse. Rain slanted, pattered on the brickwork. He shivered; he could not stay here indefinitely. But he wasn't going back. No way.

The wind dropped briefly, a lull. He thought he heard a sound, like cinders crunching underfoot. He listened. Softer footfalls, like somebody had moved off the path onto the top of the grassy bank.

Somebody was coming.

His reaction was to hide, to press himself flat against the wall the way they did in movies. He had no reason to, so he stood where he was, stared into the orange-tinted gloom.

He saw a shape, it merged into the silhouette of a man briefly before the shadows swallowed it, and he found himself tensing. He almost called out, "Who's there?"

He tried to listen but the wind gusted, buffeted the small building. It was maybe somebody like himself, out walking because he had problems. Perhaps this was a good place to bring your problems. In which case he would ignore the other, pretend that he wasn't there.

Except that whoever it was stood less than a couple of yards away from himself, a faceless outline in the darkness.

Watching him.

Maybe if Sandra hadn't done what she had, then Michael would have been apprehensive, even scared. Right now there was no room for fear in his tortured mind. Just annoyance because he wanted to be left alone.

"Who are you?" It came out as a whisper, the wind gusted it away. Probably the other did not even hear. If he did, then he did not answer.

It was Homer. Of course. For some reason the other had followed him here. Perhaps the Verger had something else to tell him which he had overlooked.

I don't want to bloody well hear it.

Or else Homer was worried about the organist, had had second thoughts about the wisdom of his revelations. Maybe he feared lest Corms might try to take his own life and his conscience had prompted him to follow the distraught man.

I don't have the courage to kill myself.

"Corms?"

The name came out of the night, had a mocking rather than an enquiring ring to it.

Michael did not answer; instead he stepped out on to the path in full view of the other. Be seen without seeing. He waited for the other to step out of the shadows.

"Shall we sing Psalm 151, Corms?"

Michael did not reply because he did not understand.

And when the lights of the distant city fell upon the face of the stranger, it made no difference whether or not the organist understood.

Because by then it was too late.

22

Sandra was shocked, not grief stricken. There was a subtle difference and Ford sensed it; it figured with the rumours he had heard. She wouldn't have wanted it this way, but that was how it had worked out and, although she would probably never admit it to herself, it solved a lot of problems.

"The children are staying with Louise." She was white faced, her hand shook as she passed a cup of tea across the table to where the detective was seated. "Louise is my sister. We're very close."

"How are the children?"

"They're okay." She made a brave attempt to smile. "Like me, I don't suppose it's really sunk in yet. I guess at a time like this you're glad your children weren't close to their father. It seems a terrible thing to say, but he never really gave them much, if any, of his time. After tea he used to go straight to the pub, usually didn't come back till midnight. Or after, sometimes."

"We're going to give you police protection," Ford said. "Just a safety measure. I don't think it will be necessary, but we can't take chances. Three organists have been killed but I don't think the killer is interested in their families."

"I'd rather you didn't." She became uneasy.

"Don't worry, you won't even notice. We did the same for Mrs Frame, and I'm sure she never even guessed. Just an officer checking the Close at night, keeping an eye on the house. It'll probably be left to the patrols. The police do that when somebody tells them that they're going away on holiday, a car will just drive by, slow down, take a look. Routine measures."

"I'm hoping to move out soon." Sandra dropped her eyes as she spoke. "Anyway, the diocese will be wanting the house." *When they appoint the next victim.*

"Oh, I see."

"I'm not quite sure when," she added, and her expression said 'I hope you're not going to ask where.'

"It's probably a good idea, Mrs Corms. Have you any idea why your husband should decide to take a walk round Stowe Pool on a dark, rainy night without even a coat to protect him?"

"I haven't the slightest idea." Her reply was curt. "There was no way of understanding Michael—he did the strangest of things. Mostly, though, he just drank. It could be that he'd been drinking heavily at lunchtime, had a hangover and wanted some fresh air. I just don't know, I don't suppose anybody ever will."

"He was all right earlier in the day?"

"I don't know. He was still in bed when I took the kids to school and he'd gone to the cathedral by the time I got back. He didn't come home for lunch; he always got something to eat out. Along with his booze. I know he sometimes went to The Scales. You could always ask there if you really want to know."

Ford nodded. "So you didn't speak to him at all yesterday?"

"No. Usually we only conversed at mealtimes in the evenings. I can truthfully say that I haven't see him for more than an hour a day, except for holidays, during the whole time we've been married."

"I believe Homer, the Head Verger, was the last person to see your husband alive, Mrs Corms. One of my colleagues questioned Homer and he said that Michael was fine, in good spirits. So for some unknown reason, Michael decided upon a walk around the pool, an impromptu decision. Either the killer followed him from the cathedral, which seems most likely, or else waited for him by the boathouse. In which case he would have had to have known that Michael was going there. Or it could have been a pre-arranged meeting. I would say categorically that your husband knew his killer."

"I really can't help you on that score, Sergeant."

"No, I don't suppose you can." Ford looked thoughtful. "Tell me, Mrs Corms, did Michael ever invite members of the choir back home? Or, to your knowledge, meet them out anywhere outside cathedral hours?"

"Certainly he never invited them back here. His social life revolved around the pubs. If you're implying …"

"I'm not, but I have to ask. I'm sorry."

"That's all right. But to put your mind at rest, Michael had no liking for children. I can't understand why he wanted four of his own, because he's never bothered with them."

"I'd better be going." Ford stood up. "If you need anything, or even just somebody to talk to, don't hesitate to give me a call."

"Thank you." She eyed him carefully, remembered James Drinkwater. The comparison was laughable. This policeman was genuine; he meant every word he said in a dutiful way. "Oh, and Sergeant …" She was nervous, embarrassed, examining the varnish on her fingernails.

"Yes?"

"I think … I think there's something you ought to know. Just in case … in case you hear it from another source and thought I was holding something back."

Ford waited.

"I've … I've been having an affair for the last few months. With the writer who lives at the other end of the Close. Gerald Norman."

"I don't think it has any bearing on the case." Ford betrayed no surprise, not so much the flicker of an eyelid. Norman had been spending time in the cathedral lately—the vergers had remarked upon it. Homer had mentioned it to Sergeant Clifford when the officer had called upon him earlier today. They needed to know Norman's motive for repeated cathedral visits. 'Research' would be the obvious excuse. It was pointless questioning Sandra Corms about it. "Your private life is your own business, Mrs Corms. I wish you the best of luck for the future."

"Thank you, Sergeant, you're most kind."

After she closed the door behind him, Sandra moved across to the window and watched him walk away in the direction of Beacon Street. Strangely, she had felt his presence comforting, a kind of feeling of safety. But in a different way from Gerry's company. The policeman was impartial but he would help if he could, she knew that. Somebody to turn to in trouble where you did not feel obligated in any way.

The sun shone briefly, turning the Close a pale golden, glinting on the golden ball atop the great central spire. The last of the fallen leaves scuttled across the sloping lawns as though fleeing from the onslaught of winter.

Sandra shivered. Not because she was cold—the central heating was full on, something that Michael would never have permitted had he been alive; the timer had always been set to an absolute minimum. Her skin prickled; another sudden shudder that brought with it a hint of fear.

Fear of what? She was revolted by that which some unknown person had done to her husband; the obscenity of the atrocity made her feel physically sick. Fortunately, somebody from the cathedral had identified the body—she thought it had been James Drinkwater. And she was grateful to the Vicar Choral for that even if she could not forgive him for his lusting thoughts on that one brief visit.

She could cope with all that. But not *this*.

Not knowing was the worst. She stood listening, fearful lest there might be somebody in the house. She heard the humming of the fridge-freezer, the ticking of the clock in the lounge. A floorboard creaked somewhere; they were always creaking, particularly in the nocturnal stillness, so they must surely creak in the daytime, too.

There wasn't anybody in the house.

Her feeling intensified, she had to fight off a surge of panic. *You're being ridiculous, it's delayed reactions. Stress.*

She wanted to run to the door, drag it open, yell for Ford to come back. *Sergeant, I'm scared because* … There was no reason to be frightened. But something was spooking her.

It was like being … *watched.*

She looked out of the window again. A few people moved about, but she couldn't recognise them at that distance. Residents of the Close, perhaps, hurrying on some errand in between the blustering showers. Or cathedral officials, coming and going from their shrine of work. Distant heads turned in her direction, looked away again. They could not possibly see her from afar.

What then? *Who*?

She thought about phoning Gerry; she might have done had she been certain that his wife was not there. Sandra was in no condition to take abuse. She wondered if he had found a place for them yet. A place of refuge.

She could not stay here alone much longer. A few days at most, and then, if Gerry hadn't found anywhere, she would go and stay with Louise temporarily.

It was as Sandra turned away from the window that a movement caught her eye. It could have been a bending of a low branch in the wind. In that brief half glance, it seemed to be part of a tree across the road. She jerked back just in time to glimpse a figure moving away. Hurrying from where he had been standing, half-hidden by the horse chestnut.

She stared, the sun glinted on the windowpane, dazzled her. She could not even be certain whether the other was male or female. An uncertain outline against a background of houses and shrubs.

She rushed to the door, dragged it open, leaned out. That mounting fear prevented her from rushing outside. Poised precariously on the top step, she clung to the rail with one hand, shielded her eyes with the other.

Now you see it, now you don't.

Where there had been a single figure, now there were three or four—she did not bother to count them. Much of a muchness, men clad in topcoats huddling together as if to shield from view the one she sought. Heads bowed, a brief muttered conversation, a chance meeting on a windswept pavement.

One turned, they all turned. Then they were moving away together, going back from whence they had come, accompanied by the one they had met; the one who had been watching her from behind the tree across the road.

They did not hurry; Sandra could easily have caught them up, overtaken them, scanned their faces. It would have been a meaningless exercise; perm any one from three. Or four. A waste of time.

An excuse because she was afraid to look upon them, fearful of gazing into the eyes of the one who had terrified her. She would not know which of them had been the watcher. *He* would know her.

She turned her head, stared up the road in the opposite direction toward the incessant flow of Beacon Street traffic. The pavements were empty on both sides; there was nobody in sight.

Ford was gone. She stepped back inside, pushed the door shut. And turned the key.

Doors would not stop him; he would find a way. If he wanted her, he would come for her. *Please, you've taken Michael, leave me in peace, let me live.*

She thought about the night ahead and prayed that the police would patrol, slow down, maybe even stop outside. And remain there until daylight came and it was safe again.

Some time later she went back through to the kitchen and made herself a mug of tea, a strong brew with an unaccustomed spoonful of sugar in it because she needed it. She almost convinced herself that her latest terror did not exist, that it was all in the mind.

Almost.

23

It was sometime after eleven o'clock when the killer let himself out into the street, moved almost furtively until he realised that he had no need for stealth. They did not know him, they could not possibly even guess. He had nothing to fear.

The storm clouds had moved on, the wind had dropped. The roads and pavements glistened wetly, a mist beginning to form. It would thicken overnight; the television weather forecaster had predicted thick fog and icy roads by dawn. Hazardous conditions.

Conditions were always hazardous.

Oncoming headlights dazzled him, for no other reason he turned his head away. Police patrols were routine, without them his ego would have been offended. They were a sign of success.

His hands were thrust deep into his pockets, his fingers closed lovingly around the bone hilt of the knife, took care not to touch the blade for it was honed to scalpel sharpness. A surgeon's implement of amputation; he smiled to himself at the thought.

Tonight he may—or may not—have use for it.

He slowed his step as he approached the Dam Street railings, saw a flock of mallard roosting on the opposite side of the pool. They quacked a guttural chorus, they had heard him, anticipating stale bread to be cast upon the water even at this hour.

He hesitated; there was no point in going up to the Close. Yet.

He thought about turning into Pool Walk, changed his mind. For no particular reason other than that a chance meeting was more likely to be remembered there than in the well-lit car park that separated the parallel streets.

There were maybe half a dozen cars parked beneath the standards with their hazy orange glow, possibly owned by late diners or cinemagoers. There was nobody in sight, no muffled footsteps heralding the approach of somebody coming to collect their vehicle.

Nobody at all.

He crossed the tarmac area, followed the exit until he was adjacent with the Arts Centre. On his immediate right was the telephone kiosk, a glass cage which destroyed anonymity. His pulse speeded up even though he had nothing to fear. Public telephones were there to be used at all hours and without question.

He stepped inside, let the heavy door close behind him.

A 50p coin was all he needed; it would not be a long conversation. Indeed, he would not speak at all. He lifted the handset, inserted the coin. His credit showed and he began to tap in the digits.

He had an infallible, retentive memory, so he did not need to consult a number written on a scrap of paper which might have been used in evidence against him. He had looked it up in the telephone directory at home, committed it to memory.

3 … 9 … 0 … 6 … 9 … 2

A pause. A faint *click*. Now it was ringing out at the other end.

He found the sound almost musical. Erotic. His fingers went back to the knife handle and rubbed it softly, sensuously. Memories came, he didn't try to shut them out, distracting as they were. Because they were exciting.

The old man first, Herbert Poppleton. He had writhed weakly, died quickly. Too quickly.

Rupert Frame had been stronger, hands clutched to his groin in a futile attempt to staunch the blood loss. The killer had had to slash his victim's throat to silence the screams.

Corms had been the best, the most satisfying. Out there by the boathouse there had been no one to hear his cries. The killer had let him run, stagger; it had been so funny that he had laughed as he watched. And Corms had *known*, recognised his attacker; he had also known deep down that he wouldn't live to tell.

He had made maybe ten or fifteen yards before he had collapsed on the cinders, kicked his last, and his bloody fingers had come away with something clutched in them.

That had had the killer writhing, too. With pleasure. The fury had returned later.

The phone was still ringing out.

Lastly, he remembered the girl. It was funny that she should come to him now, but he didn't mind. Just a painted picture, but she was more erotic than any woman he had ever seen in the flesh. Seen, not had, because that pleasure had been denied him throughout his life. By them—Poppleton and his kind—they had made him what he was. And they had paid for it.

Now it was time to rectify that, to indulge in those delights that had never been his in his enforced celibacy.

His fingers gripped the handset, threatened to crack the plastic. *Answer, you bitch!*

The girl in the picture mocked him.

You cow, I know you're there.

He found himself starting to count the ring-outs. Eight, nine … eleven …

He hooked the receiver back, heard his coin drop down, fumbled beneath the flap to retrieve it.

Outside the mist was thickening faster than predicted. He was tempted to go on up to the Close. He stroked the knife in his pocket again.

No, not tonight. Tomorrow, maybe, or the night after. There was no hurry. He stepped out onto the pavement, turned in the direction of the car park.

The girl in the picture was calling him. Right now he needed her more than the real thing. She had really excited him. He quickened his pace.

24

"I've already told your colleague everything I know, Sergeant." Charles Homer's tone was one of annoyance; he was not in the habit of having visitors to his small terraced house adjacent to the Close.

"I need to know more about Herbert Poppleton." Ford was unruffled. Again his keen sense of smell picked up that bachelor aroma, the stale odour of a house that lacked a female touch. In contrast with Cecil Clay's bungalow, Homer's abode had an air of permanent untidiness about it; clothes were draped over chairs, dirty washing was heaped on the unswept floor by the twin tub. The windows were small, a low wattage unshaded bulb created a depressing gloom.

"He was the best friend I ever had." A note of defiance, challenging the other to dispute it. "He found me this job and he kept it open for me until I returned from my TA service."

"Perhaps he had no choice." Ford's voice was low, almost threatening.

"I beg your pardon!" Homer stiffened in his chair, for a moment there was a flicker of fear in his eyes. He swallowed.

"You met in Essex in 1957." Ford's features were expressionless. "At the time you ran a sadism and masochism establishment until police investigations caused you to close it down. Herbert Poppleton was an occasional client of yours. There was a scandal; you needed to move away so you followed Poppleton to Lichfield. Your wife had already left you; you needed a job and somewhere to live. You *persuaded* Poppleton to fix you up with both of these. Had his secret life of perversion become public knowledge he would surely have lost his job. His marriage would have folded, too, had his wife even suspected his involvement with S&M."

"This is preposterous!" The Head Verger's attempt at indignation lacked conviction. The colour had drained from his features, his clenched hands had begun to tremble. "I've a good mind to write to the police complaints department …"

"Let's not be silly about it." Ford sighed, thrust his hands deep into his pockets. "You don't want to dig up skeletons any more than I do—for me it's just a waste of time. I can prove what I say, I can only suspect that you were blackmailing Poppleton, or at least holding the threat of exposure over him to keep your job. I don't want to go into that, I just want a few facts which might help me."

"What do you want to know?" Homer slumped back in his chair, his brief show of bravado gone.

"I want to know about the choirboys whom Poppleton invited back to his house."

"I don't know any details, he never told me."

"But you've a good idea who went there and what went on."

The other nodded. "Yes. Herbert had a liking for young boys—I knew that from the time I first met him. I knew only too well what went on up at his place, his wife was blissfully unaware of it. I just hoped he didn't get caught; my job would have gone as well as his. At the time the cathedral hierarchy didn't like me, for no particular reason that I could put a finger on. Herbert had his little naughty games he used to play with the boys, he used to start off by suggesting they sang Psalm 151. That was the cue. I think he made it all seem like a joke, a bit of fun."

"Do these names mean anything to you?" Ford produced the register of pupils from his pocket, opened it up, and passed it across to Homer. "That's the list of choristers there."

"Hmm." Homer held it at a distance, sucked his lips. "Clay, I remember him, he used to go round to Herbert's place. A strange boy. And Drinkwater, a sad case. His parents were both killed in a car accident whilst he was at school. No other family except two brothers who were at boarding school somewhere. It would have had a devastating effect on James had Herbert not taken him under his wing. He was like a father to him. Sometimes the boy stayed with him and his wife during the school holidays. But maybe it would have been better if he hadn't."

Ford's eyebrows rose slightly. He waited.

"From a happy-go-lucky boy James Drinkwater became an introvert, a loner. I tried to convince myself that it was the shock of losing his parents that made him that way but I know it was Herbert's influence that did it. A kind of enforced celibacy, at least where the opposite sex was concerned. Herbert had never looked at another woman in his life; I think he indoctrinated James against them. After he left school, Drinkwater just drifted away, I don't even know if he kept in touch with his mentor. Then he turned up again after Poppleton had retired as Vicar Choral. I suspect either Herbert recommended him for the job or else he used Herbert's name as a lever. But nearly forty years hadn't changed James, he was still a loner, a strange bloke, and I guess it wasn't any surprise when he got together with Clay."

"You didn't like Frame." It wasn't a question this time.

"The feeling was mutual. If he could have come up with a legitimate reason to get me the sack, he would have done so. I've run the cathedral my way for many years, he wanted to interfere, wanted changes. He wanted a Head Verger he could dominate."

"And Corms?"

"He was all right, apart from his drinking. But neither Frame nor Corms were in the same mould as Herbert Poppleton—they weren't fit to shine his shoes!" There was an obsession in the way he spoke, almost a fanaticism in those staring eyes. "He didn't deserve to die the way he did, though."

"He was disturbed the last time he left the cathedral, wasn't he?"

"No, he was fine. Absolutely fine."

"I think you're lying, Mr Homer."

"Look, I didn't really notice, I just saw him leave, locked the door after him. He seemed all right."

"I'll take your word for it." *Because you're living in the past, in your mind Herbert Poppleton's still here, up there in the organ loft for services and practices. And you hate anybody who might have usurped him.* "Thank you for your help, Mr Homer. I may need to talk to you again."

Hero worship, in excess, was a dangerous state of mind. Idolisation was only a step away from hatred; the borderline was a narrow one. For Ford, it was a worrying thought.

* * * * *

"I had a phone call last night." Sandra's obvious relief at seeing Ford turned to concern. "About eleven."

"Oh?"

"I didn't answer it, I just let it ring out. I thought it was never going to stop. In the end it did. I checked, rang my sister in case there was any problem with the kids. It wasn't her calling. Nor somebody else it could have been, I checked with them this morning."

"It might just have been a wrong number." Ford's hunch said it wasn't.

"No." She smiled weakly. "I know it wasn't. I could tell. A woman's intuition, if you've heard of that. I don't expect you to understand."

"I get hunches, too. I have a golden rule: always play your first hunch. It's invariably right—later ones often fudge your reasoning."

She told him about yesterday, the feeling of being watched, her terror. "It sounds silly, you must think I'm foolish."

"Not at all." His expression was serious.

"You're as worried as I am."

"Just playing careful. The patrols check the Close out

three times during the night hours but I think maybe I ought to keep tabs on you, as well. I'll phone you tonight, after ten. Three rings and then I'll call back. Okay?"

"Fine. By the way, I should be moving out, probably Friday, like I told you I might. My boyfriend's found a place, a cottage belonging to a friend who's working abroad for a year. Kinver, if you've ever heard of it."

"I have, a lovely location." A stone's throw from Malvern. "You'll love it there."

"Gerry's down there now. He's staying there until I join him on Friday."

Ford had been meaning to talk to Gerald Norman but maybe it didn't matter any longer. "I'll buzz you tonight."

He debated whether or not to confide his suspicions in Borman. He decided it was too early yet; the chief wouldn't listen to gut feelings. Some guy was killing organists because of what one perverted old man had done to him, made him. Revenge was complete but there was one pleasure in life that the killer had been denied by his own hang-up. There was an urge to satisfy it, maybe just curiosity, a burning desire to step outside celibacy.

The killer wanted a woman, and who better to satisfy his lust upon than the widow of one of his victims?

Ford went cold at the thought. He prayed that Sandra Corms would survive the night hours.

25

The killer stepped out into the street. Tonight was vastly different from the previous night. For a start, he was two hours earlier; the cathedral clock was just beginning to strike nine and there were people about. Not crowds, just a few couples on their way down to the Cornmarket Carvery; a bunch of youths who looked like they might be going to McDonald's.

This morning's fog had cleared by lunchtime; there was too much of a breeze for it to return. The last of the leaves rustled and scuttled in the gutter, farther down the street somebody kicked an empty drink can, sent it rolling and clanking.

A high-pitched whine followed by a multi-coloured explosion over Minster Pool. Ducks quacked in alarm; some took off with fast, whistling wing beats. The first firework of November had disturbed them. Another couple of nights and they would take no notice.

There were maybe fifty cars on the car park, clustered in bunches of four or five around the lamp standards. Light deterred those on nefarious business. The killer instinctively skirted the brightly lit area. People would recognise him if they saw him; there was no reason why he should not be abroad in the city at this hour. But they might remember having seen him. He was not taking any chances. He never did, which was why he still walked free.

The same route as the previous night brought him to the telephone kiosk at the car park exit. He glanced at the glass cube, but tonight he had no need of it. Last night she had not answered but he knew she was in. The ringing had frightened her; he smiled to himself at the thought. Phoning tonight would only serve to warn her that he was coming.

For her.

The sight of the phone booth kick-started his memory. The escalating thrill, what it had done to him as he stood there fingering the knife in his pocket. But he had waited, had not succumbed to temptation. He knew it was only a matter of time. In the meantime, the girl in the picture had partially satisfied him.

At the height of his lust he had driven the blade into her, hacked and gouged the paintwork. He had heard her screams in his frenzied brain, he had shown her no mercy. He had pushed himself to the very limits of his physical endurance, his brain had seemed to explode in unison with his sweat streaked body. A moment of unbelievable bliss before he had blacked out.

When he had regained consciousness on the cold floor, he smelled blood. Like Herbert Poppleton's blood. Rupert Frame's. And Michael Corms's. He felt its sticky warmth on his fingers, raised his arm so that he could stare at it. It fascinated him.

She had bled just like the others, and that was incredible. He licked at it with his tongue, tasted its salty, iron flavour. It made him feel heady, euphoric.

It was a bitter disappointment to discover that he had nicked the palm of his own hand with the knife blade. A bitter disappointment. But logically, he could not expect her to bleed.

But the sensation had been beautiful whilst it lasted. Now it was over, and he was the way he had always been. Mean. Hateful.

Hating them for what they had done to him, for making him this way. Which was why he had never had a woman other than the girl in the painting. Tomorrow night, he promised himself, he would have flesh and blood.

Her flesh first, quivering and jerking beneath his own body, moaning her pleasure aloud.

Then her blood, gushing thick and scarlet out of her wounds, still lying beneath him. Her moans would turn to screams.

Then she would die with him still lying atop her, and he would relax on her corpse until that feeling of ecstasy was gone.

When he would become mean and hateful again.

He would take her to the place he has in mind first, though. Because only there would he be able to erase the scars of everything which *they* had done to him. The slate would be clean; he would have no remorse.

He had not thought beyond that. Afterwards it did not matter.

Nothing mattered once he had had *her*.

Beacon Street was busy, a constant stream of traffic in both directions. The headlights dazzled him so that when he turned into the Close he had to stand and wait whilst his eyesight adjusted. Here he felt vulnerable, he knew that he must hurry.

The cathedral was floodlit, unusual for a weeknight in the autumn. He took a deep breath, exhaled slowly. Perhaps they had switched on the illuminations in his honour. Because he had come to offer a human sacrifice, an offering to appease their God for the sins that had taken place within His house. Retribution for making him what he was.

It was as though the brief rest had revived him, reassured him. Now his movements were quick and lithe, positive. He knew what he had to do and how he would do it. He felt the hilt of the knife throbbing in answer to the pulses in his hand.

She *was* at home; a shadow passed across the curtain. His other hand went to his pocket, delved deep until it found what it was seeking; for one awful moment he thought the key must have slipped down into the lining. It felt small and hard in his sweaty palm as he squeezed it.

Her front door key. A duplicate. She would not have missed it because she was confused by the death of her husband. She wasn't grieving; she might even welcome his coming in her loneliness.

But he did not want her after tonight. She would have served her purpose by then. As well as his own. He wondered what it was like to lie with a woman; the thought of the experience had him lusting, eager. He could not wait any longer.

The key fitted perfectly, turned noiselessly. He had to use his shoulder to push the door open, held his breath as it scraped on the centuries-old warped floorboards. But the music playing behind the closed door of a room leading off from the hallway drowned out any noise he might make. He closed the door behind him, locked it in case anybody should chance a call.

There was no longer any need for stealth.

His fingers closed over the handle, depressed it. The door swung inwards noiselessly. He stood there looking in.

Sandra had not seen him; she was totally oblivious to his presence. The small lounge had sparseness about it, the stacked cardboard boxes and the tea chest piled with newspaper wrapped objects bespoke a pending departure.

He was only just in time.

She was sitting in an armchair with her back towards him. The stereo was playing a country and western tape. His lips curled in contempt for her taste in music, it was deplorable. He would not want her after tonight.

Her head was bent forward; she was dozing. He edged around until she came into full view. Oh, God, she was beautiful!

As beautiful as the painted girl, and he had destroyed her, too.

She wore black jeans and trainers, a t-shirt that showed her cleavage. Her breasts excited him.

His one hand was still thrust deep into the pocket of his topcoat, the knife handle was slippery with his sweat. He was fully aroused; he could wait no longer.

Suddenly, the telephone in the hallway rang. He started, dragged the knife from his pocket, held it at arm's length, the blade barely a foot from her exposed neck.

The phone rang three times then cut out.

She stirred restlessly but her eyes remained closed. That dreadful cheap music played on.

"The highway she's hotter than nine kinds of Hell."

It grated on his nerves, and he resisted the temptation to kick out at the stereo, smash it. Silence it.

She was big and beautiful. *More* beautiful than the girl in the painting.

Then the telephone began to ring again. And kept on ringing.

He almost screamed at it to be silent. But it wasn't as harsh as that cheap singer on the tape.

"When you're down to your last shove with and nothin' to sell."

This time her eyes opened. She saw him, stared uncomprehendingly.

The telephone was still ringing, insisting to be answered. Nobody was going to answer it.

Recognition dawned in her frightened eyes, widened them. Her full lips moved, mimed something because the words would not come.

The telephone continued to ring and the singer sang on. The killer was not listening to either.

He had to shout to make himself heard above the noise, words that came instinctively. "Shall we sing Psalm 151?"

It was some seconds before he realised that the telephone had stopped ringing. He reached out with his free hand, jerked the stereo plug out of its socket. The sudden silence was almost deafening.

Sandra didn't scream. Not because the tip of the knife blade was only inches from her throat. Simply because she had only the strength left for a whisper. One word that was barely audible.

"*You!*"

26

Ford did not leave CID Headquarters in Rykneld Street until after nine. Borman had called a meeting following a press conference. Stalling because they had not come up with anything positive and they had to be seen to be doing *something.* Corms's killing had made fools of the police. Not just *The Mercury*, the nationals, especially the tabloids, were loving it. They had their scapegoat, Borman was looking for his.

It hadn't been a good meeting. Ford was glad to get out. In the central office he played a hunch, picked up the phone.

"Explaining to the wife why you'll be late home again?" Clifford ribbed him but Ford wasn't listening.

Three rings the other end and now it was ringing out again.

Still ringing out.

Sandra could be in the bath. Or on the loo. He let it ring on.

"She's maybe got fed up waiting in, night after night, Jason, and gone out. Wives won't stop home forever, you know."

Serena, Ford's first wife, hadn't. He didn't want to think about her, it was too painful. Right now he only had thoughts for Sandra Corms.

Shit, she wasn't going to answer! Finally, he dropped the receiver back on to its cradle.

"You'd better hurry home, Jason."

He left the office at a fast walk, oblivious of the laughter that followed him. Out in the station car park he gunned the Fiat's engine and squealed the tyres. He screeched them to a halt in Dam Street, two minutes, twenty seconds later. The traffic lights at the top of Tamworth Street had not been in his favour otherwise he could have made it twenty seconds sooner. He dared not shoot the lights.

Drinkwater's shop and flat were in darkness. Ford

debated briefly with himself, got out of the car and tried the street door.

It was unlocked.

The shop smelled of musty books. The untidy living quarters reeked of stale sweat.

He saw the slivers of wood on the bare floorboards, the gouged pieces of pine that had once been varnished and painted. The girl's face on it was barely recognisable, just wide eyes that stared up in terror at him.

Oh, Jesus Ford, just look what he did to me!

His keen eyes saw the bloodstains on the dark boards; the wood had absorbed them but he knew only too well what they were. He was certain that the lighter stains were semen that had dried.

Ford's blood ran cold. He should have played his hunch earlier. It was too late now.

He hesitated for one moment, thought about radioing for backup, changed his mind. This was his show, he owed it to himself. Reinforcements would be no help, it was one against one from now on. He had a personal score to settle, he had something to prove yet again.

He ran down the stairs and out into the street, ran all the way to the Close. He wished that he had drawn a pistol from the armoury but that would have entailed explanations to which Borman wouldn't have listened. The Chief Inspector played everything by the rulebook.

Lights were showing in Sandra's house. And for the second time within a space of ten minutes Ford found a door unlocked.

Drinkwater had been here. And gone. And he had taken Sandra with him.

He searched the house. He knew he wouldn't find her but his training was instinctive. Running up the stairs, throwing open bedroom doors. A mean machine that refused to panic.

Nothing. Just like he had expected. Downstairs he checked the lounge again. There were no signs of a struggle;

Sandra had gone meekly with her captor. Doubtless at knifepoint. *The* knife.

Ford went back outside, stood on the steps. A dilemma, whether or not to call for backup. Self-recrimination because he should have confided in Borman, raised the alarm. It was too late now. Time was running out, he could not afford to wait for reinforcements.

'Abducted women and children are usually dead within the hour.' One of Chief Dawson's sayings, spoken with a lifetime's experience. Oh, please God, let this be the exception.

Ford took a deep breath, held it, put himself inside the killer's mind. A victim, still alive. He needed a place to do what he had to do to her, somewhere not too far away, somewhere where he would not be disturbed.

Stowe Pool? Corms had died there, nobody had heard his screams. It was a possibility. The Detective turned his head, saw the cathedral illuminated by the floodlights. Majestic, it humbled you, was representative of the Almighty in all His grandeur. A holy shrine.

A sacrificial altar?

He did not hesitate, made straightway for the west doors. He knew they would be locked, his intuition told him that before he tried them. It also told him to check out the north transept entrance, the one that the clergy and choir used. The one that Homer locked and unlocked like some sinister guardian of the gates of doom.

The door creaked slightly, swung inwards to his touch. Inside, the nave and choir stall lights burned softly, the aisles were in blackness. Ford's fingers closed over the torch in his pocket. There must be a duty Verger somewhere; surely the cathedral would not have been left unsupervised at this hour.

It had been that time when Frame had been killed.

Ford moved forward, walked on the balls of his feet, he remembered how the echoes gave you away. Again, he regretted the absence of backup. There were a thousand places in which the killer could have hidden, in which a mutilated body could lie undiscovered. It might take hours of searching. Man hours. He was only one man.

Time was running out fast for Sandra Corms.

He would check on the Verger's office first, perhaps the duty man worked there with bowed head, oblivious of all else.

Ford resisted the temptation to shine his torch, if the one he was seeking was in here then he must not reveal his presence. He crept stealthily down the north aisle.

Suddenly he stumbled; almost fell, as his foot caught against something lying in his path. Even in his stagger, he whirled, flicked the torch switch. God Almighty!

He had sensed by the brief contact that the obstacle was human. Unconscious. Possibly dead.

The inert body was most certainly dead, smiled up at him with its gashed throat, dribbled fresh blood. Legs drawn up in a final agonised writhe, slippery, scarlet fingers clawing at the wound in one last futile attempt to staunch the flow. The features were awash with blood, eyes bulging, threatening to burst.

Possibly the open mouth had screamed once prior to the attack, a shriek that had been drowned in a torrent of arterial blood. Recognition was not easy, Ford had to bend over the corpse to be sure. At first he had presumed that it was Drinkwater. It wasn't.

It was Charles Homer.

The policeman caught his breath. Clearly the Head Verger had come to investigate an intruder and had paid for his curiosity, his devotion to duty, with his life.

Which meant that the killer and his victim were inside the cathedral.

Ford moved swiftly, stealthily, flitted from pillar to pillar. In the reflected glow from the choir stalls he saw the organ loft above, a cluster of pipes that gave it an altar-like appearance in the half-light. *A sacrificial altar.*

He moved at a half crouch, made it to the steps,

mounted them. The balcony was a river of blackness, a miniature Styx in this place of death. His nostrils flared, he thought he scented blood. It was his imagination; his life, Sandra's, depended upon realism.

The loft was empty.

He turned back in disappointment but not for a second was his vigilance relaxed. The hunt must continue.

Back down in the nave he hesitated briefly. He must check out the small chapels, the Lady Chapel and the Chapter House, St. Chad's and St. Stephen's. For tonight there would be no holiness in any of them.

A noise, a movement. Ford froze, tensed, his eyes searching the gloom and shadows. It had come from over there, across in the south transept.

It creaked again.

He glided on the soles of his shoes, recalled again how Homer had died, a crooked arm aloft to protect his throat. It was icy cold in here, outside the wind had risen as if to mask any sound which an ambusher might make.

Ford followed the wall around until he reached the south door. It was locked, nobody had passed through it. He felt on with an outstretched hand until he came to the corner, slid his flattened body round it.

That was when he almost fell through the low, small doorway, his weight pushing the heavy studded door back, iron hinges creaked their protest. The frame barely reached his shoulders, it would be necessary to stoop low in order to pass through. Like the entrance to the domain of some evil dwarf.

In his mind Ford envisaged a pit or dungeon, a deep hole where Cromwell had cast his Royalist prisoners after the siege, a damp and airless place where they had died and decomposed, now only their whitened bones littering the floor. A feeling of vertigo, clutching at the woodwork in case he, too, fell down there.

Cautiously, he flashed his torch, an on-off movement, a split second of pencil beam that revealed all he needed to know. Fresh air wafted his face, came down the spiral staircase that wound on up into the blackness above.

And Ford knew, without any doubt, that that was where James Drinkwater had taken Sandra Corms. That somewhere up there was the altar of his perverted fantasies upon which he intended to sacrifice her.

27

Sandra was having difficulty breathing. It was a combination of shock and the physically exhausting, seemingly never-ending climb up this spiral staircase inside the great central spire.

It was all a terrible nightmare, it had to be. She had fallen asleep on the settee in the lounge and the bad dream originated from that awful lusting visit of Drinkwater's that time when he had called on the pretext of congratulating Michael upon his appointment as organist. Her husband's murder hadn't helped. She hadn't grieved, you only did that when you loved somebody, but she had been devastated by the sheer horror of it.

She hated James Drinkwater for what he had done. She also pitied him because he was mentally ill. Most of all, though, she feared for her own life.

She would wake up soon, find herself back in the lounge, surrounded by boxes packed in readiness for her leaving. She couldn't wait to get away; from the Close, the city itself. It was all one awful bad dream.

It wasn't. It was reality, the hand that stretched up from a couple of steps below, touched her bottom through her jeans, was flesh and blood. The very same hand that had wielded the knife which had cut out Homer's throat in a single blow.

She knew that her captor carried that knife in his other hand, he would not hesitate to use it if the mood took him.

"I … can't … go any … farther." She leaned on the stone wall; her legs would not hold her up much longer.

"You can and you will!" He seemed scarcely out of breath. "We have some way to go yet. The spire is two hundred and fifty-two feet high; it commands unrivalled views of the city and its surroundings. I climbed it once before, when I was a chorister. I was fourteen then. It was a special treat to come up here and I've never forgotten it.

You will be enthralled when you look out from the top window."

The very thought brought on a sense of vertigo. Only the reminder of that bloodstained knife prevented her from sinking down on the steps. Somehow she remained standing. "Can't … can't we rest … just for a moment."

"All right." That hand came around her and she stiffened when the fingers squeezed her breasts through her jacket. "Just for a minute." Because there wasn't any hurry, nobody would think of looking for them up here. She probably would not be missed until tomorrow, and even then they'd think that she had just gone out somewhere. The alarm might not be raised for twenty-four hours.

By then it wouldn't matter.

"Why *me*?" She couldn't stand the silence, the sound of his regular breathing. A shaft of floodlight through one of the arched windows slanted on his face. Sandra shuddered; she had difficulty recognising the Vicar Choral. Gone was that vague expression, the musician's absent-mindedness, his obsession with the great masters to the exclusion of all else; in its place was a much more intense look, one that terrified her.

"Because," his thin lips stretched, his eyes seemed to burn in the reflected light, "you are beautiful."

She trembled, feeling physically sick.

"I've never had a woman." His voice seemed far away, like it whispered up from the stairwell down below. "They denied me that. Poppleton and what he stood for. Young boys are nice and safe; they don't cause you problems. I never did anything to a boy, either. You believe me, don't you?" He was insistent, pleading, seeking a positive answer.

"Yes, I believe you."

"Clay is just like me, we pitied each other in our own way. You know Cecil, don't you?"

She didn't, but she said she did.

"His only real pleasure came from a girl in an oil painting, and he only found her a few months ago. I know how he felt—I had a painted girl for years, she was beautiful. Just a face on a piece of varnished wood, not just the face, the *eyes*, they saw and they understood. They seduced you. Tonight I killed her!"

Sandra started.

"I had to kill her to make way for you." There was a sadness in his tone now. "I didn't want to, but it was the only way. She haunted me; I could tell by the expression in her eyes that she knew I was going to find another woman. She tried to stop me. That was why I killed her. So that I could have you."

Sandra did not answer this time.

"Cecil still has his woman. He killed a man to make room for her. A painting, a portrait. The chap bore a likeness to old Herbert Poppleton. Cecil hated Herbert, too. Herbert made him what he is today, just like he did me. But Cecil never had the guts to do anything about it. *I* did!" His voice rose in pitch. "Not just Herbert—though he was the worst—but those who came after him. Because they're all alike, and if they aren't, they soon will be. I had to kill them to save other boys from suffering what I suffered, from becoming like me. You do understand, don't you?"

She didn't, but she said she did. It would be dangerous to argue with him.

"I've always liked you." His tone was softer now, he shook as though he was nervous, embarrassed, a teenager on a first date. "I've watched you from a distance a lot lately. You've been unfaithful to your husband."

"Yes." It made her feel guilty now, far worse than ever before.

"I wanted you. Badly." His head dropped, she could no longer see his expression. "I knew this was the only way. I hate that writer, I've watched him mooching in the cathedral lately, I thought perhaps he suspected that I had feelings for you. I thought about killing him, too."

Her legs wouldn't hold her up much longer; she was fighting to stand upright.

"You have sex with him? Of course you do. Tell me about it, tell me what you do."

"I … I …"

"You're embarrassed." His head came up and he smiled apologetically. "Never mind, you can tell me later." His tone changed; there was an urgency in it. "We must press on."

She climbed a step at a time, dragged one leg behind the other. His hand rested on her bottom as if he was afraid that she might fall back.

Her ears popped, the vertigo returned, spasms that came and went. They passed another window and she turned her head away so that she couldn't see outside. Often in the past she had stood in the Close and gazed up at the main spire, watched the sunlight glinting on the golden ball. Even that used to make her dizzy. It was an awful long way from the ground.

She had to rest again. This time he did not complain, just stood behind her and smoothed his hands up and down her buttocks. Those fingers attempted to edge between her closed thighs, so she began to climb again.

Her heart was beating crazily, there was a roaring in her ears, and she had to breathe consciously. Far below, outside, she heard the hum of distant traffic. City nightlife continued; it would never stop. No matter what James Drinkwater did to her.

Another sound, so faint it was almost inaudible. She thought for a moment that Drinkwater had stumbled, maybe stubbed a toe. A careless footstep. Except that it seemed to come from the stairway down below.

A desperate hope was raised within her; it was all she had left, even if it was soon to be dashed. It was something to cling on to even if it was futile.

Sandra began to sob with relief. Somebody was following them up here.

28

Ford moved as fast and as silently as possible. He did not need to use his torch; the glow that filtered inside gave him all the light he needed. Through one of the lower windows the glare of the spotlights was dazzling.

He ran. Stopped. Listened. Ran again. Oh God, they had to be up here somewhere!

Another landing; the stairs wound on into the gloom. He paused to listen again. Somebody was talking, a man's voice. Then silence.

Now Ford knew that Drinkwater and his prisoner were not far away. The detective's relief was overwhelming but he could not afford to relax. There was no way of knowing when the killer would strike; the only certainty was that he would, sooner or later. Ford prayed that it would be later.

On and on, Ford's calves began to ache. He wondered how Sandra was faring. It was her mental ordeal that worried him most at this stage. The damage could be irreparable.

Suddenly, he saw them. They stood maybe fifteen or twenty steps above him on what must surely be the summit landing. He rounded a bend in the twisting staircase and quickly stepped back into the shadows. They had not seen him, and by the way Drinkwater was threatening Sandra with a knife, Ford could not afford to let his presence be known.

"Take your clothes off." The command was spoken softly, a thousand times more menacing than if James Drinkwater had screamed it in a frenzy. So cold and calculated, like how a GP might ask a patient to prepare for an examination.

"I … I …" Sandra was shaking, leaned back against the wall; she looked as if she might slump to the floor at any second.

"*Take … your … clothes … off.*"

A slight movement of the killer's outstretched hand, the point of the blade pricked her throat. She tried to scream, but it came out as a strangled gasp. In the half-light the watcher saw how her terror-stricken features were bathed in sweat.

Then she was pulling at the zip on her jacket with shaking fingers. It snagged, she tugged it free.

"Come on, hurry!" Drinkwater urged.

Ford eased around the corner, dropped to his hands and knees, hoping that the shadows would hide him if he kept low.

"I've never had a woman, you know. I think I told you that." The Vicar Choral was shrugging out of his topcoat, passing the knife from his right hand to his left. He tore at his trouser belt. "They deprived me of that."

Ford's expression was grim. Anywhere else he might have laughed at the sight of James Drinkwater, trousers around his ankles, trying to kick his feet free. But not here. The situation became more dangerous by the second.

Ford wished that he had a pistol—he could have picked Drinkwater off without hesitation. But he didn't have a gun and wishful thinking was negative.

He crawled up another step.

Sandra was attempting to drag her jeans down. Her quivering legs finally gave way and she fell backwards. There was a grunt of pain as she hit the hard floor.

"Get up!" Now it was a shout.

"I … can't." She sobbed, lay there, her back resting against the wall.

Drinkwater stooped, grabbed at the jeans. There was a ripping sound and they came away in a rush, throwing him back. He staggered, regained his balance, stared at the whiteness of her legs.

"Lie there, spread yourself!" His whisper was heavy with lust, he tore his shirt from his body, regardless of buttons, shredded it so that it dangled from one arm. "Now …"

Ford made another two steps. Another yard and his

outstretched hand would be within reach of the other's bony ankle. Sandra's eyes were closed, her head back. She had either fainted or else had resigned herself to the most terrible fate a woman could suffer.

Drinkwater knelt down, fumbled with the lower regions of his body. He grunted, a sound that embodied anger and frustration. Despair.

"Bitch!" he hissed.

Sandra's eyes were open and she was staring up at the spiral roof, seeming to have divorced herself from awful reality. She wanted to get it over and done with. Maybe she even wanted to die.

Drinkwater was back on his feet, and when a shaft of light washed over his face, his expression was terrible to behold. His eyes were bloated, the pupils rolled, his hands clawed the air in agonising realisation. A shriek, a cry of defiance, mumbled obscenities frothed out of his mouth.

Ford stared in disbelief; he did not understand. Sandra was looking, cowering, an arm flung up to protect herself, fearing a frenzied attack. But the uplifted knife fell from those fingers, clattered to the floor.

"Look! Look, in the name of God, this is what they did to me! They denied me even at the last!"

Had Ford moved then he would have had his man, taken Drinkwater's ankle, toppled him, overpowered him. But he held back. Not just because the danger was gone, but because he didn't understand. Two seconds, maybe three, and then it was too late.

In one move, a twist and a bound that belied the stiffness of that naked body, James Drinkwater leaped for the unglazed arched window. Somehow he secured a hold, dragged himself up, crouched on the narrow ledge. A living gargoyle that screamed his hatred for those who had made him thus, cursed them for the pleasures they had denied him.

Perhaps he saw Ford, perhaps not. He gave no sign, seemed to roll forward, a bather on a springboard bracing himself to meet the water below. He did not scream as he went, a silent shape that was lost from the view of the watchers.

"You're safe, Mrs Corms." Ford went to Sandra, knelt by her side. "He's gone. He won't be coming back."

She looked up, smiled weakly.

There was a faint *thud* somewhere outside.

Ford squeezed her hand reassuringly; in a moment he would go and look outside. There was no longer any hurry.

"I'm okay," she whispered. "Honest."

"You were very brave, Sandra." Her first name rolled from his tongue before he realised it. It didn't matter. "You stalled him all the way."

"No." Her voice was husky; perhaps at the end she pitied the wretch his inadequacies. "I don't think it would have made any difference, there was no way he was going to be able to do what he wanted to do."

"Maybe not." Ford moved away from her, crossed to the window.

Outside the floodlights were bright, showed up every detail of the magnificent architecture right down to the roof of the south transept. The tapered spire thickened until it joined with four smaller turreted spires. Upon one of these a tiny shape hung like a rag doll, barely recognisable for what it was. Arms and legs swung limply. James Drinkwater was finally at peace.

Ford turned back, making an effort to appear relaxed, even casual. "Can you make it down if I help you?"

"I'll try." She used an arm to lever herself upright. "He couldn't make it, you know."

"I know." Ford slid an arm around her waist, let her lean on him. "The one thing he wanted most in life, but when it came to it, he couldn't manage it. A painted picture on a piece of wood was the nearest he ever got, and he even destroyed that. In the end there was only one place left for him to go."

He felt her sobbing on the lengthy descent; crying was

best for her right now. She had to get it out of her system.

His own thoughts turned to the chief. Somehow Borman would claim the credit. That was okay by Ford; he didn't expect anything else.

In the end, it really didn't matter a damn.

ABOUT THE AUTHOR

I had my first story published in a local newspaper at the age of 12, followed by 55 more before I was 17. It was a good start to a writing career and I owe much of it to my mother (historical novelist E.M. Weale) who gave me every encouragement. My father, though, was insistent that I followed family tradition and went into banking.

Hence it was twenty years later before I became a full-time author and I had some catching up to do. The 1970's were a boom time for pulp fiction and I made my debut with 'Werewolf by Moonlight' (NEL 1974). It was 'Night of the Crabs', though, which really established me as a writer, virtually overnight in that memorable record, hot summer of 1976. This title was the 'No.1 beach read'. It saw numerous reprints, spawned 6 sequels along with several short stories, as well as a movie.

'Night of the Crabs' enabled me to go full-time. At the time with my wife, Jean, and our four children we were living a reasonably conventional life in Tamworth, Staffordshire. It was time to move on though, and in 1977 we moved to our present home in a remote part of the Shropshire/Welsh border hills.

I was no stranger to country life though, and the further away we were from town and traffic the better. For many years I had been writing for the 'Shooting Times' and several other sporting publications. Then in 1999 I accepted the post of Gun Editor of 'The Countryman's Weekly'. This involved 4-5 articles per week and I relished the challenge.

By this time pulp fiction was virtually out of fashion so diversification suited me, yet my readership has remained faithful to me and technology has made it all possible again with e-books. Thus my backlist is almost completely returned to electronic print along with some new books. It is an exciting time.